THE LAST
FIELD PARTY

Also by Abbi Glines

THE LAST FIELD PARTY

A Field Party Novel

BY

ABBI GLINES

SIMON & SCHUSTER BFYR

NEW YORK   LONDON   TORONTO   SYDNEY   NEW DELHI

SIMON & SCHUSTER BFYR

An imprint of Simon & Schuster Children's Publishing Division
1230 Avenue of the Americas, New York, New York 10020

Jacket photograph of background by MAVERICKZ85/
SHUTTERSTOCK; jacket photograph of couple by SUMMER
LOVEEE/SHUTTERSTOCK
Jacket design by Laura Eckes © 2022 by Simon & Schuster, Inc.

For information about special discounts for bulk purchases,
please contact Simon & Schuster Special Sales at 1-866-506-1949 or
business@simonandschuster.com.
The Simon & Schuster Speakers Bureau can bring authors to your live
event. For more information or to book an event, contact the Simon &
Schuster Speakers Bureau at 1-866-248-3049 or visit our website at
www.simonspeakers.com.
The text for this book was set in Stempel Garamond.
Manufactured in the United States of America
First Edition
2 4 6 8 10 9 7 5 3 1
CIP data for this book is available from the Library of Congress.
ISBN 9781534430969
ISBN 9781534430983 (ebook)

To every high school librarian and teacher who put this series in the hands of your students, and to my two oldest daughters, Annabelle and Ava, who are no longer in high school. The two of you inspired every one of my stories. Events in your lives and lessons you learned through your teen years gave me fuel for my imagination. Without the two of you, this series would have never been created.

THE LAST
FIELD PARTY

FIVE YEARS LATER

ASA AND EZMITA

"You didn't completely walk away from Asa Griffith's truck that day."

CHAPTER ONE

ASA

I slid the last box into the back of my truck. I was leaving Mississippi with a hell of a lot more than I had arrived with five years ago. Choosing to redshirt my freshman year due to Covid had given me more than just one more year of eligibility to play. It had given me more time to build a life here. Glancing back toward the building that had been home for the past three years, I smiled thinking of all the memories that had been made here. Dex and Joe had been not only my roommates but my teammates as well. They were the first two friends I had made my first year at Ole Miss. Dex had been my roommate in the dorms freshman year. We had been together the longest.

Dex was already gone. He had been a top pick in the NFL draft and would be playing defense for the Patriots. Joe and I were the only ones left to move out today. He was going back to Texas to work on his family ranch. It was what he had always known he would do. Like me, football had been a way to pay for his education. I had known after my first year I wouldn't be NFL-bound.

Deciding on a degree and what I wanted to do with my life hadn't been easy. I had changed my mind a few times. In the end, I had chosen to major in Spanish. Teaching Spanish in high school while also coaching high school football was my goal. My advisor had suggested I major in history, since that was where my strengths were.

In the end, I had chosen Spanish because it made me feel closer to *her*. Over the past five years, I had spoken to Ezmita twice in person while we were both in Lawton for the holidays. It was never for as long as I wanted, but then she was never alone. Facing the fact she had moved on was one of the hardest things I'd done.

"Yo! Griffith! You want this toaster?" Joe called out from the door of our first-floor apartment.

I shook my head. "No."

Joe held it in his massive hands, turning it over and looking at it a moment. "It's beat to shit, ain't it?" he then added.

I nodded in agreement. He shrugged and walked back inside with it. Knowing Joe, he would take it anyway. He rarely threw anything in the trash.

Unlike Joe, I wasn't positive where I would be in the fall. I had two options, and I knew I was real damn lucky. Not everyone was leaving with two job offers. Choosing Spanish as my major had been one of the smartest things I'd done while I was in college. Seems that high schools are looking for Spanish teachers that can also coach football teams. Starting with Lawton High School. However, neither school was offering me a head coach position, and I didn't expect one. Just because I had played for an SEC team didn't mean I was ready to take on a high school team.

Lawton was offering me a special teams coaching position along with a Spanish 1 and 2 teaching position, which came with a very good salary. I would be coaching with Nash, and that would be awesome. However, as many good memories as I had at Lawton and on that field, there were bad ones too. As dark as you could fucking get.

Then there was a 5A high school just outside Atlanta offering me an offensive coaching position along with the Spanish 1 teaching position. The salary was higher, but so was the cost of living in that area. However, looking at it as an outsider, the Georgia offer seemed like the obvious choice, and I was leaning that way.

I still had two more weeks before I had to make a decision, and during those two weeks I would be able to find
my closure in Lawton. The fear that I would choose it for
the wrong reasons weighed on my mind. The timing of
things was perfect. In two weeks, the field owned by the
Lees would be named in memory of our former friend and
teammate Hunter Maclay.

Maclay Field would no longer be a field in the woods
where the teenagers went to party. Those days were over.
They had been for the past few years. The parties ended
with us. It was time to make the place that had played such
a big part in our lives something important. Nash and Ryker
Lee were doing just that. Maclay Field would host football
camps all summer with former SEC players and NFL players as special coaches throughout the summer sessions. I
was signed on to do two weeks in July.

Profit made from the camp would go into the Hunter
Maclay Scholarship Fund to be awarded to one Lawton
Lion senior every year. In addition, each youth who wanted
to attend the camp but could not afford the cost would be
eligible to receive a Hunter Maclay seal of approval that
would pay all costs for that child.

Ryker and Nash had spent the past year working on the
program and turning the field into a field for young kids to
learn the game of football. The Maclays had also put a lot

of money behind the project and worked with the Lees to make this something to benefit Lawton and leave a legacy for Hunter.

The official opening ceremony would be open to all of Lawton, and the high school band was going to play. There would be food vendors, fireworks, and special speakers. However, the night before it would be a smaller gathering. Those of us who grew up on that field would be going one more time to spend a night remembering the moments that changed us forever.

The sound of the apartment door swinging open and banging loudly against the side of the building broke into my thoughts, and my head snapped up to see Joe once again standing at the door. He was so big, he filled the doorway, and the sight made me smile. I would miss him.

"You not gonna take the damn hair dryer either?" he asked, holding up a pink hair dryer.

"Joe, when did I ever own a pink hair dryer?"

He looked at it as if he was just now realizing its color. Then he shrugged. "I like pink," he finally said.

"Then you keep it. I think one of Dex's Exes left it here a year or so ago," I explained.

Joe smirked. He loved referring to the list of women Dex had dated as Dex's Exes. It didn't take much to amuse Joe. He was always so damn happy and ready for a laugh.

That was an energy I would miss being around every day.

"I'll take it to Gerti," he said before going back inside.

Gerti was his younger sister. He had five younger siblings, but Gerti was the only girl. His entire family always came for the home games. I had gone out to dinner with them more than once over the years. They reminded me of families I had watched on sitcoms growing up. The kind I hadn't believed existed.

One day I wanted a family like Joe's. A wife who loved me and a shit ton of kids being loud as hell. Smiling, I walked back to the apartment to say good-bye before heading back to Lawton.

CHAPTER TWO

EZMITA

As I stepped inside my parents' store, the smell of cinnamon rolls engulfed me, and I smiled. Home. It had been months since I'd smelled Momma's famous cinnamon rolls. I didn't realize how badly I needed to be here until this moment. When my mother's small body came rushing from the back door to greet the customer and her eyes locked on mine, my chest tightened. A lump formed in my throat, and unshed tears stung my eyes.

"Hey, Momma," I said, sounding as emotional as I felt.

"Ezmita!" Momma cried out with joy and opened her arms wide as I hurried into them.

"I missed you," I whispered as she hugged me tightly.

"You stayed away too long this time. But you are here now. Let me feed you. You're too thin," she said, pulling back and looking at me. I said nothing as she studied me. It only took a moment, and then she nodded. "I see," she said. "Come, then. I will send your sister to watch the front and you can tell me how you broke things off with Malecon. It was time."

I wasn't surprised my mother knew without my having to tell her that I had finally ended my four-year relationship. She always knew. It was her gift in life. She read the minds of her children, or at least it felt that way most of the time. "Can I have a cinnamon roll?" I asked her, craving the familiar taste.

"I have conchas in the house kitchen. Chocolate ones, just like you love," she told me. "I woke this morning, and my spirit, it knew you were coming."

Perhaps it was God or one of the many saints that talked to Momma, and she didn't read our minds after all. Whatever the reason, I was thankful. At least today. Conchas, my momma, and home were exactly what I needed right now.

"You eat many because you have lost too much weight," she told me. "TERESA!" Momma yelled for my eighteen-year-old sister. She was the only daughter they had at home now. Rosa attended Saint Mary's in San Antonio, Texas, and lived with Momma's older sister and her family in the summers there. They owned a restaurant that had become well-known in Texas, so it stayed busy. Rosa worked as a waitress, and she enjoyed living in Texas. I missed her terribly.

Teresa came from behind a new shipment of boxes that hadn't been opened and stocked yet. "What, Momma?" she asked, then her eyes met mine and she squealed with delight before running toward me. I barely had time to catch her in my arms when she threw herself against me.

"EZMITA! You're home!" she cried out and held on to me so tightly it was difficult to breathe. I was sure this affection was due to the fact she missed me but she also missed Rosa. I knew Rosa hadn't been home since Christmas. I spoke to her often on the phone.

"Missed you too," I replied. The smile on my face was genuine and needed. Just coming back here made all the hard stuff fade away.

"Are you staying all summer? Can we go shopping? Will you stay in Nashville? Can I come visit? Will you be here for my graduation this Friday?" She began drilling me with questions as she leaned back to look at me but didn't release me just yet. It was as if she were afraid I would disappear.

"Not sure. Yes. Not sure. Yes, wherever I end up. Of course," I replied. "Did you honestly think I would miss the first Ramos to walk across the Lawton Lion field and get a diploma?" I asked her. Both Rosa and I had been homeschooled. I was thankful Teresa had been able to experience high school.

She grinned brightly. "I am a first, aren't I?" She was proud of that.

"Yes, you are. Momma and Papa are getting lax in their old age," I teased and winked at Momma.

She scowled at me, but I could see the twinkle in her eyes. Having almost all of her kids home made it difficult for her to be angry. "That is enough chatty chat for now. Teresa, you go watch the store. I need to feed Ezmita," Momma said and continued on walking toward the house entrance.

I gave Teresa's hand a squeeze. "We will talk tonight after work is over," I promised her. "I want to know all about the hallways of Lawton High."

She nodded happily, then hurried on to the front of the store.

"Your father will be back from the bank soon. He knows you're coming. He will hurry," Momma told me as we walked into the house.

"How did he know I was coming?" I asked.

She glanced back at me over her shoulder. "I told you, I made the chocolate conchas this morning," she replied as if I were daft.

"Oh, right," I said and bit back my smile. It is so odd now to think there was a time only a few years ago I'd wanted nothing more than to get away from my parents and this place. Now, as I walked into the door of our home, my heart was healed. I felt whole again. It was as if Momma's arms and these walls held magical powers to fix me.

"Momma," I said, stopping as I closed the door behind me and inhaled the smell of home. Tears stung my eyes once more, and I struggled to keep from crying.

"What is it?" she asked me.

"It's good to be home. I missed you and Papa," I said, unable to find the words to express all the emotion in my chest.

"Oh, Ezmita. It will always feel that way when you return. It's okay to cry. Happy tears are those that built these walls," she said and reached up to gently pat my cheek. "Now come eat."

Laughter bubbled from my chest as tears fell onto my cheeks. "Okay, Momma," I replied.

Walking through the hallway and into the kitchen, I saw our memories hung on the walls. Family portraits taken every year along with baby pictures of all the Ramos kids. I couldn't remember the last time this wallpaper had been anything different than the blue flowers. That once annoyed me, but now I cherished it. I found comfort in it.

"Sit," Momma instructed as I walked into the kitchen.

I did so, and she began making me a plate of food. It would be far too much food, but I would eat it all to make her happy. Seeing her had made me happy. How odd growing up was. You went from wanting your momma as a child, to wanting to get away from her as a teen, to wanting her yet again as an adult.

"What thoughts have that smile on your face?" Momma asked as she put a plate of chocolate conchas and a serving of mixed berries sprinkled in sugar as if I were still five in front of me.

I looked up at her. "The truth?" I asked.

She nodded her head.

"You," I told her.

CHAPTER THREE

ASA

Nash had offered to let me stay at his place while I was in town, but I had needed somewhere I could escape to in the evenings. I had decisions to make, and being back here in Lawton was enough to mess with my head. I wasn't the same kid who left here five years ago, and I had a decision to make that would impact the rest of my life.

Besides, Nash had his own house now, and there were several people coming into town that might need a room. I'd leave his three-bedroom house available to them. It was more house than Nash required, but he'd finished college in three years by taking summer classes, gotten his teaching degree in physical education, then gotten hired full-time by

Lawton High as not only an offensive coach but a phys ed teacher. He made a nice salary for a single guy.

I winced at the idea of Nash single. I hadn't been back to Lawton since he and Tallulah broke things off a year ago. I didn't know all the details, but she had been offered a great opportunity in Chicago as an intern. They had done the long-distance thing until she had hooked up with her new boss or something like that. I wasn't sure.

Putting my duffel bag on the white king-size bed, I walked over to the window. This was a new hotel. It had been built three years ago. There was nothing fancy about it, but it was clean with big rooms. It also sat diagonally across the street from the Ramoses' store. Moving the curtains back, I saw what I had expected when I walked into my room and realized which way it was facing.

My view was the Ramos Stop and Shop. Great. Just what I wanted to look at every day I was here. Shaking my head, I walked over to the minifridge to take out a water that the guy at the front desk had said would be inside it. Along with the water were three chocolate bars, a bag of trail mix, and two apples. I grabbed an apple and bottle of water, then went to sit down on the chair beside the window.

Might as well look at the damn place and get it over with. Once I got my mind off Ezmita, I could focus on my future. She wasn't a part of that. I used to measure every girl I dated up against her, and they failed. It took me until my third year in college to stop doing that. I still didn't have any serious relationships, but at least I could date a girl more than once.

Damn if Ezmita Ramos wasn't gonna be my girl that got away for the rest of my life. I took a bite of the apple and stared at the store. I recognized a few faces as they filled up their cars with gas or went inside to get groceries. Being back here was weird. It didn't feel like home. Not with my mom buried in the cemetery. I hadn't spoken to my dad in five years. Last I heard from Ryker, my dad was living in Little Rock. His momma was real informed by the gossip mill in town. It was believed that my father was also remarried.

I was the reason we hadn't spoken. He had tried to call me a few times over the years, but I never answered. He had sent me a handful of letters that I never opened. Eventually he stopped. It was how I wanted it. I preferred a world where my father did not exist.

My thoughts didn't get much further about him. Standing up, I walked closer to the window. My eyes locked on the girl I hadn't thought I would see. But there she was walking outside carrying a bag of groceries for Gran Lee, Ryker and Asa's grandmother. Even from here I could see that damn smile that still haunted me in my dreams. Hell, it haunted me in the daytime, too. When I least expected it, Ezmita would always show up in my thoughts.

Last time I had asked, which had only been a few months ago, Nash said she was still in Nashville after graduating college. He hadn't known much more than that, but I didn't expect him to. Her hair was shorter, but it looked good on her. She looked older, like a woman. Not the young girl who had broken my heart.

It had taken me a while to accept that she had been right. That day in my truck, she had chosen what was best for her and in the long run best for me. I'd been ready to do anything to get her to come with me. To choose me. In the end, Ezmita had chosen herself. She had been more mature at eighteen than any girl I had dated.

The last time I had seen her, she had been holding hands with a tall guy who was speaking Spanish because he was talking about the night before when they had been making out in the stockroom of her parents' store and her younger brother caught them. The guy had tossed Ezmita's bra over the boxes to hide it from her brother and they still hadn't found it.

Ezmita had been laughing up at him so hard that she was wiping tears from her eyes. Until she had turned and our eyes met. Her laugh faded, and then she had just smiled.

She had greeted me and asked how I had been. Small talk that people who once knew each other did before going their own way again. She hadn't known I was fluent in Spanish and I'd understood every word of their conversation. Nor did she know that my chest had felt as if someone had fucking kicked it. I drank a six-pack of beer by myself at the field that night.

There was no sign of the guy with her now. I had returned to this town for closure. Ezmita was the biggest part of that closure. I needed to be able to put my past firmly behind me in this town so that I could decide which job to take with a clear head. Reaching for my wallet and the key card to the room, I headed for the door.

Once I was outside the front of the hotel, I scanned the parking lot for Gran Lee's Buick and found it pulling out onto the road. I turned my attention back to the parking area and found Ezmita just as she was about to walk back inside the grocery store side of the Stop and Shop. Someone called her name, and she paused and looked back to wave. It was then her gaze moved and she saw me walking across the road and in her direction.

The bright sun made it difficult to see her expression so I could gauge how this was about to go, but I knew Ezmita well enough to know she'd wait for me to reach her. I saw her move toward me then, and as I walked under the shade of the awning I was able to see her smile. That damn smile still did things to me.

"Asa Griffith," she said, looking happy to see me. "I didn't expect you to be in town, but then again, I didn't know about the field dedication. Mrs. Lee just told me about it. She's so proud of it and what the boys are doing. It sounds amazing."

Her voice was the same. She was the same. Just older and more appealing. Which wasn't fair. God could have helped me out and let her age badly. Although my feelings for Ezmita went far beyond her appearance. It had been much deeper than that.

"Yeah, it's gonna be great," I said realizing how much of an understatement that was. "I'm here for the dedication, and I'm doing two of the camps in July," I added then.

She still had to tilt her head back to look up at me. I always loved the way she did that. "You were the first one I thought of when Mrs. Lee told me who would be doing the coaching. I was hoping I would run into you. It's been a couple years."

"Two," I replied too quickly.

Her smile, however, widened. "Yeah, I guess it has been. Time goes so fast now, doesn't it? I mean compared to when we were younger. I feel like I blinked and college was over."

I nodded once. "Yeah, I know the feeling. Are you back

here for a while, or do you live in Nashville now?"

Her smile fell a little, and she didn't have a quick response. I wondered if there was something important I was supposed to know. Had someone died and Nash not told me? Damn, I hope I didn't ask the wrong thing.

"Right now, I honestly don't know," she finally said.

I let out a small relieved laugh. "You sound like me," I replied.

For a moment, five years hadn't passed. We were still the same two people we had been that summer before college began. We had the world before us and so many plans, so many dreams. Then the door to the store opened and Mrs. Ramos called out, "Ezmita! I need you to get back to the register."

She glanced back at her mother and nodded. "Yes, Momma. Coming." Then she turned back to me. "I better get back in there. It was good seeing you, Asa. Take care," and she walked inside with one last wave. The illusion was gone.

CHAPTER FOUR

EZMITA

Weren't people supposed to stop growing when they hit puberty? Wasn't that how it worked? Because holy crap, Asa was massive. He had not looked like that the last time I saw him. Just two years ago, he had been broader, maybe taller, but he had not been the huge brick wall that he was now. The very wide, muscular, towering, gorgeous, brick wall . . . ugh! I shook my head at my thoughts.

I had told myself I would not think about Asa that way. Although it was hard not to think about him being gorgeous when he was absolutely just that. He was this big, huge man now, and crawling up that brick wall sounded way too appealing. *STOP IT!* I scolded myself.

Asa was a former SEC football player. I had been surprised when he didn't go into the NFL draft, as had been my brothers. Everyone in town had expected him to. He had settled on a career instead. I wondered if he had been hurt or if it was because of a girl. There had to be a female. A guy did not look like that and remain single.

Tall, leggy models with long flowing hair and tiny waists that turned heads everywhere they went were what you found on the arms of a guy like Asa Griffith. There had to be one somewhere around here that belonged to him.

I had made the right decision five years ago. I was not the kind of female that dated guys like Asa. Nothing about me was supermodel material. We were grown now, and the teenage years were over. All just fond memories to cherish.

I shoved all thoughts of Asa aside and focused on talking to the customers as I rang up their groceries and bagged them. There were very few new faces. Most I had known all my life. They had been coming in here as long as I could remember. By the time we closed the doors that evening, I knew all the town gossip and updates. More information than I wanted to know.

Taking off my apron, I tossed it into the dirty bin, then picked up the bin to take back to the laundry room.

"What did the Griffith boy have to say?" my mother

asked me as I walked into the house with the dirty basket from the store.

"Just to say hello," I replied with a shrug.

"He is a big man now."

I laughed then. "Yes, Momma, he is rather large," I replied.

When she said nothing more I started toward the laundry room with the basket.

"Is he staying in Lawton?" she asked me.

Stopping, I sighed and shrugged. "I don't know. We didn't talk that much. I dated him briefly five years ago. I don't know him anymore." And that sad fact was one I wished I hadn't verbalized. Knowing something and stating it aloud were two different things. The latter hurt more.

I put the aprons and towels into the washer, then headed for the stairs. I knew dinner would be ready soon. I could smell the mole and knew we would be having chicken tonight. Teresa had been gone all afternoon to a senior picnic the school had hosted. She still wasn't home, and I knew it had to do with either a boy or the fact she didn't want to work in the store.

Either way, I knew she would be home soon, because missing family dinner was not acceptable.

I wanted a moment of peace in the room I was sharing with her before she returned and talked nonstop about her day. I would be happy to hear about it, but for just a few minutes I needed to talk myself back into a good mood. Somehow I had gotten into a funk, and I feared it was over Asa freaking Griffith.

The fact I could so easily be put in a funk over a guy I dated one summer five years ago when I hadn't shed a tear over a relationship that ended after four years said a lot. Too much. More than I needed to know about how much time I had wasted with Malecon. The worst part was he had loved me. He still did. He had told me at least once a week that he loved me for the past three years, and not one time had I been able to say it back.

Yet he had stayed with me. He had stayed with me until he had given up on us. I had stayed with him because Malecon was my friend. He was comfortable and safe. I didn't have to worry about a broken heart with him because I hadn't given him mine to break. When I had first met him, I'd instantly disliked him.

He had been working at our store as a stock boy, and I had been fixated on Asa. I had overlooked him or just been annoyed by him when he made it impossible to ignore him. That had been our way up until the day I had walked away from Asa Griffith. I had decided letting him go was the safest and smartest thing to do for myself.

When I had walked into the store and gone directly

to the back of the store to break apart and cry, it had been Malecon who came to sit beside me. For the first time he hadn't talked and said stupid things. He had been quiet. He had let me cry, and when I was ready he had listened to me ramble on about all that had happened.

Over the next year, he became my best friend.

Then he became more than that. He had followed me to Nashville. We had just fallen into a relationship. It had seemed simple. Like it was expected. As if it had been what was supposed to happen. But deep down I had known I could never love him the way he wanted me to. I did try, though. I did.

His final words to me had been "You didn't completely walk away from Asa Griffith's truck that day. You left part of yourself behind. I can't keep waiting on you to get it back."

Until today I had thought those parting words were ridiculous. I had told myself Malecon had wanted to hurt me because my not being able to love him had hurt him. So he went after something in my past he remembered that had broken me, but I was over that. I was a grown woman now. I had even called him immature for bringing it up.

Now, I wasn't so sure if there wasn't some very tiny bit of truth to his words. I did not think I left a significant part of myself behind with Asa. That would be insane. I had moved on, gotten a degree, made new friends, found a new life. I rarely thought of him. Well, maybe once or twice a week. But that was normal. He had been my first love and sadly my only love.

The door swung open and banged against the wall as Teresa came rushing inside. "I need help! I need an excuse to get out of this house tonight. There is this guy . . ." She began to prattle on so quickly I only caught bits and pieces of what was said. My own problems continued to plague me while I tried to follow along with Teresa's.

I wasn't sure, but by the time we went down to dinner I thought I might be a part of a plan to leave the house after dinner to go to the drive-in movie with her, although she wouldn't really be watching it with me. I doubted our parents believed this, but then she seemed certain they would. I decided I would go along with it. Besides, who doesn't like to go to the drive-in and watch a movie alone?

CHAPTER FIVE

ASA

Trying to get my mind off Ezmita I spent the rest of my day visiting some friends. It was just before eleven when I pulled back into the parking lot of the hotel. Nash had ended up inviting over several people to his house, and we had ordered Chinese food and sat in wooden Adirondack chairs in his backyard around a metal firepit drinking beer like middle-aged men. It had been nice.

Ryker and Aurora had arrived in town last week to prepare for this weekend's events. With Ryker now playing for the Cowboys, it made it harder for him to get back to Lawton regularly, but his plan wasn't to stay in the NFL long. Just a few years, then he wanted to come back and settle down in Lawton. Aurora hadn't come to Nash's with Ryker. No one brought a girlfriend with them, and I wondered if that was because of Nash's single status, but I didn't ask.

I was walking across the parking lot when I saw headlights pull into the Stop and Shop and then park around the back beside the house. It wasn't my business who it was, and it was late. Ezmita had sisters who could drive by now. I kept telling myself that, among other things, but instead of continuing to walk toward the hotel entrance, I turned and walked across the street.

The car lights were still on as I crossed the empty street, and I could see a definite female getting out of the driver's side door. I made longer strides, and just when I reached within a few yards of the car, I heard voices and realized the driver wasn't alone.

"If we are caught, they can't ground me. You realize that? This is all on you," Ezmita said.

"We were at a movie," the other female voice replied.

"No, *I* was at a movie. I don't know what you were doing," Ezmita said.

She was with her sister, I realized. I didn't know which one. I stepped under the security light so they could clearly see me before speaking. "I hope it was a good movie at least."

Both heads spun around and looked at me with wide eyes. Ezmita didn't look scared, just surprised. She would have recognized my voice. Her sister, however, began to curse in Spanish, then asked Ezmita if I was there to see her.

"Go inside, Teresa," Ezmita replied to her sister. "And try not to get caught," she added in Spanish this time.

Teresa studied me closely a moment, then smiled as if she approved before doing as her sister told her. Before she went inside, she called out, "You need to make this one stay. He's much better than the last one. He's a brick wall of sexy!" She said it in Spanish.

Ezmita rolled her eyes and waved a hand at her sister as if to shoo her off. Then she swung her gaze back to me. Those eyes hadn't changed. The way she could look at me, and I felt like she knew me.

"You're out late," she said once we were alone.

"Just got back from Nash's. How was your movie?"

She shrugged. "Popcorn was the best part. They always put too much butter on it," she replied.

"I haven't been to the drive-in since . . . well, since that summer," I admitted.

She smiled and shrugged. "Me either, until tonight. Seems my sister has a crush on the quarterback. Apparently the girls in this town can't seem to stay away from the football players."

"You should warn her," I said.

"Oh, trust me, I tried," Ezmita replied, then smirked at me.

Damn, this was nice.

It was also confusing as hell.

"How long are you here for?" I asked her, needing some kind of closure or reason to stop thinking about her being a part of Lawton.

She sighed, and her shoulders lifted and fell with the action. Her gaze went back to her house, then back to me. "I don't know," she finally said.

That was not helpful. Not in the least. I didn't need the temptation of Ezmita Ramos being in Lawton. I had a decision to make about my future. My career.

"What about you? Are you leaving after this weekend?" she asked me.

That was a loaded question. One I had hoped would be easier to answer. "I don't know yet," I replied.

She grinned at me, then laughed softly. "How is it we are college graduates and this confused about our current situations? Shouldn't we be settled down in jobs and know what we want by now?" she asked.

I nodded. "Yeah, you'd think so," I replied, not wanting to admit that I had two job offers and it was me standing in the way of that settling down. My inability to decide.

"I never expected to come back here, you know? I thought once I got out that I wouldn't want to come back except to visit. But now that I'm here it feels like the most stability and comfort I've had in a while," she said as she stared up at me, her eyes full of so many emotions. Several I understood.

"I think there is a country song about that," I teased.

That got another laugh from her. "Probably several," she replied, then glanced back at the store behind her. "I don't want to work here. That's not it. I just feel less lost being near my family, being in Lawton. I think I've been lost for a while now, and I didn't even realize it."

When I had walked across the road to talk to Ezmita, this conversation was not one I had expected; however, I wasn't against it. Perhaps having it would help both of us.

"Lawton will always be your home. Your family is here. It makes sense for things to feel right here," I told her.

She gazed up at me silently for a few moments. "What about you? Is it your home?" We both knew what she was asking with the unspoken words. My home life here hadn't been like hers. The only warm memories I had were made by a woman who was buried six feet under. My mom had given me what she could until she couldn't any longer. Even those brief moments of happiness were jaded now with the truth of what she had endured by my father's cruelty.

"I don't know," I finally replied. Because there were times this was home. My friends were here, my childhood was here in this town, but was it enough to make this home?

She nodded as if understanding.

"I hope you find your home one day, Asa Griffith," she said softly, then smiled up at me so sweetly, I felt it in my chest. Damn. I wish she didn't have that ability still. "I need to get inside before Momma comes out here looking for me," she said. "Good night."

I didn't want this to end. For five years, she had been the one thing that stayed on my mind. The one girl I couldn't forget. Seeing her again was not helping me. "Good night, Ezmita," I replied, and I stood there and watched her until she was safely inside before heading back to the hotel.

CHAPTER SIX

EZMITA

Going to sleep thinking about your first love when you're twenty-three and waking up doing the same thing is rather pathetic. Perhaps it is normal, though. All part of coming home and facing the past. Getting the closure and living the new life you have made for yourself. I was going to tell myself that anyway.

Waking up in the same bedroom as my sister was nice for a visit, but this wasn't permanent. I couldn't move back in with my parents. They would always meddle in my life. I was used to my privacy now, and I needed that. I looked down at my phone and read over the e-mail from the principal at Lawton High School one more time.

When I had sent in my application I hadn't truly thought I would get a response so quickly. I had figured I had time to think about moving back here or putting in my application at other places. It had been my sophomore year in college that I decided I wanted to be a teacher. It had taken me several more months to decide I wanted to teach history and I wanted to teach high school.

My parents had surprised me by being behind this decision and then went on to tell me what good benefits and retirement being a teacher had. None of which had been why I had decided to become a teacher. It all came down to: I was good at it. I had been teaching my younger siblings my entire life. It was second nature to me. I knew I could do it and I could do it well. I also enjoyed history. Learning about why we are who we are today and how we got here.

Until six months ago, I had planned on applying at high schools near and in Nashville, but things had begun to change with Malecon and me even before it was over. My thoughts had begun to move toward whether I would want to stay in Nashville after graduation if Malecon and I ended things. Did I truly want to stay there if we didn't?

Now here I was back in Lawton with my degree and teaching certificate, and an interview four days after applying for the position. I hadn't even told my parents yet. I had told no one. They would be thrilled. They would assume I

would be living under their roof. I would have to explain
that I had money saved up and would be renting a place of
my own.

My parents weren't going to understand that at all.
Not when their house was right here in town. I wanted to
put that argument off for as long as possible. It could be
pointless. I might not even get this job. Just because I had a
degree didn't mean a high school principal was going to hire
someone who had never attended a public school herself.
Having been homeschooled might present an issue for me. I
wasn't sure yet just how much of one it would be.

I'd had four years of college experience after having
missed the college admissions deadline my first year after
graduating. I had done some online classes until the following January, when I finally got to move away. I hoped that
counted for something. Momma was already at the store,
and the smell of her cinnamon rolls filled the house, mean-
ing she must have had to bake some in the house kitchen as
well. I listened for any sign of life before making my way
downstairs. If one of my family members saw me dressed
in this straight navy skirt that hit right below the knees,
white blouse, navy heels, and pearls, then they would know
something was up.

The house was silent. Stopping in the kitchen, I found
a plate of cinnamon rolls left out, and I knew they were for

me and whoever else came along. I grabbed one and poured a cup of coffee in a go cup, then hurried to the door to get out of the house before I was caught. If they saw me after the interview, it would be fine. Then I would be done with it and I could answer the million questions they were going to hammer me with.

I glanced back in the rearview mirror at the store as I pulled onto the street, knowing my momma had to see me leaving and wondering if she saw me walk out to the car. There was a good chance she had. It was hard to slip anything by the woman. I shoved all thoughts of my family aside and took a deep breath.

I was a grown woman. I had my first real interview for my first job in my career choice. This past semester had been my last step to being certified. I had successfully finished my student teaching at a 5A high school in Nashville. This was it. I was a big girl now.

My pep talk continued the rest of the five minutes it took for me to drive to Lawton High School. It wasn't nearly as large as the high school I had done my student teaching at, and I loved that about it. When a school was too big it was almost as if it were a university, and there was no way to know everyone. You met strangers daily, and many you never crossed paths with again. Here it would be different.

I parked my car and looked up at the brick building I had once wanted more than anything to attend. Simply so I could know Asa Griffith. Rolling my eyes at the shallowness of my youth, I reached over and picked up my purse from the passenger's seat along with some sample projects I had been given an opportunity to try during my student teaching.

Not everyone gets as lucky as I had when placed with a teacher for their student teaching. Jane Harmond had been teaching history for over thirty years. She loved her job, and she loved trying new things. Anything to get the kids attention away from their "gadgets," as she would say, and focused on their learning. Jane had become my mentor and friend. Leaving her had been harder than leaving Malecon, and that said way more than I wanted to admit.

Walking up to the front entrance of the school, I hoped the office was easy to find. The e-mail hadn't given me instructions on where it was located. Most people in Lawton had stepped foot in this building at one time in their life. Most, except me.

"You might be the last person I expected to see walking in those doors this morning," Asa's voice drawled, something so similar to what I was thinking it took me a moment to realize he was real and not in my imagination.

Turning around, I found Asa behind me with a pleased yet intrigued expression on his entirely-too-sexy face. This was not what I needed before I walked inside for my interview. Being professional was important. I wanted to make a good impression. Being all flushed from seeing Asa Griffith in a sleeveless white tank that was sweaty and sticking to his chiseled chest was not going to help me accomplish that.

I refused to let my gaze continue down his body, although I could tell he was wearing shorts of some kind. "Uh, yeah," I stammered. "Good morning." I had forgotten what it was he said to me. Dang him for looking like that. Why couldn't he be less attractive? Life was not fair.

"Good morning," he replied with an amused grin now playing on his lips. "You heading inside for some reason in particular?"

I glanced back over my shoulder. Telling Asa about my interview wouldn't hurt. He wasn't my parents, and he wouldn't want to discuss it. This didn't affect him. "Yeah, I have an interview. I should probably get going. Don't want to be late."

I could see that surprised him, but then Asa and I knew little about each other anymore. He had no idea what my degree was in or what my plans for my life had become. He only knew the unsure girl from five years ago. Just as

I didn't know what he had majored in and where he was going. All I knew was he hadn't gone into the NFL.

"Good luck," he finally said.

"Thanks," I replied, then hurried to get inside the doors in case I couldn't find the office, not once thinking I could have just asked Asa where it was. Neither of those things mattered, though. The signs were right there, and the office was steps away from the entrance. I paused and took a deep breath, regaining my composure and focus. Running my hands down the front of my skirt, I straightened the fabric, thankful it wasn't the kind that wrinkled.

This was it. This would determine if I stayed in Lawton or if I found my new life somewhere else. No pressure, Ezmita, I whispered to myself, then made my way inside the office door.

A woman in her midfifties with red hair cut into a short bob looked up from the desk she was sitting at. Jewel-framed glasses were perched on her nose, and she had on bright red lipstick. When she smiled, some of the lipstick was on her teeth. "Good morning, you must be Ezmita Ramos."

"Yes," I replied.

She stood up and walked over to the counter separating us. "I'm Henrietta Horn. I work summers in the office and help out some during the school year too. Let me go tell Mrs. Campbell you are here," she told me, then walked down a small hallway that I assumed led to offices behind her.

That had been easy enough. Henrietta had been pleasant. I glanced down at the folder in my hand and wondered if this was too much. Perhaps I should have mentioned it to Mrs. Campbell before just bringing this with me. No, I was overthinking things.

"Ezmita," a voice said, and my head snapped up from the folder I was studying in my hand. A tall lady with platinum hair cut short above the ears stood where Henrietta had been earlier.

"Yes," I replied.

The woman smiled then. "I'm Belinda Campbell, please come on through the opening just there and we will go back to my office and get to know each other," she told me.

I did as she said, all the while wondering how someone could be so captivating and in command yet not raise their voice or speak in a tone that demanded it. Belinda Campbell had a talent. I felt as though if she snapped her fingers a line of people would come to attention.

"Excuse the smell. It's rather strong. They cleaned the carpets this week, and although they are dry for the most part, the smell of cleaner is still lingering," she told me as she turned and led the way down the short hallway past

Henrietta, who stepped out of the way and gave me a small nod before going back to her spot in the office.

I had been so focused on the interview I hadn't noticed the smell until now. "My mother overuses cleaning products daily. I hadn't even noticed," I replied.

"Your parents own the Stop and Shop," she said. It was a statement, I realized, and not a question. She had done her research on me. "On Fridays I treat myself to a cinnamon roll before coming in to work. It has put about five pounds on me this past year, but I feel as if it is worth it."

We entered the office at the end of the hallway. "Please have a seat," she told me, waving to the two plush royal-blue chairs across from her desk. She didn't go sit at the chair behind her desk, but she sat down in the royal-blue chair closest to the wall.

"I moved here last year from Arizona. It was an adjustment for me. Your mother has been very helpful more than once with ordering items I went into the store looking for that she didn't have in stock. Several times I went in on Friday, and she had three dozen cinnamon rolls set aside for the faculty. You have generous parents."

Those things didn't surprise me. That sounded like something my momma would do. I nodded. "Yes, I am very lucky."

Belinda smiled. "Now, tell me, Ezmita. Why history and why high school students?"

I hadn't known what kind of questions I would be asked, but this one I was prepared for because I had asked myself the same thing when deciding what I wanted to do with my life. Settling back in the chair, I placed my folder in my lap and began to tell Belinda Campbell just that.

CHAPTER SEVEN

ASA

Unable to stop being curious about Ezmita's interview, I turned back and headed toward the field house, where I had left Nash. He had picked me up this morning from the hotel to work out with him and the team, but I had planned on running the six miles back to the hotel. That was going to have to wait.

It was empty except for Nash when I returned. Nash was the youngest coach, which meant he was the one with the responsibility to be here every morning to see who showed up and make sure they worked out properly. At least during the summer months. Workouts weren't mandatory, but if you wanted a chance to start in the fall, you came every morning at six. However, with school having just let out last week, I could see in their eyes this was the last place they had wanted to be today. That would change the closer the summer grew to August, and real practice would begin.

Nash was inside drying off from the shower when I walked inside. His head shot up, not expecting someone, which was obvious since he was barely clothed. The relief in his expression when he realized it was just me was comical.

"Thought you left," he said.

I nodded. "Yeah, I was, and then . . ." I paused, not sure how to say this without making it seem like I cared. Which I did, but not to the degree Nash was going to assume. "Uh, I saw Ezmita Ramos."

Nash nodded his head once, then dried his hair before pulling his shirt over his head. "Yeah, I heard she's interviewing with Ms. Campbell for the history position," he replied casually. As if this were no big deal. It shouldn't be. It was just that I hadn't even known Ezmita had gotten her degree in history or that she had decided to be a teacher.

"Ms. Campbell is the new principal," I clarified, making sure that was who he was referring to. When I had been given my job offer, it had been through Coach Rich. However, my meeting would be with the new principal and Coach Rich. It was a chance for me to ask questions about the job and find out details that hadn't been explained yet.

Nash nodded. "Yep" was his only response as he continued to stare at me. I could see the smirk in his eyes even if it wasn't on his lips yet. He was fighting it.

"I've seen her a couple of times since my return, and she never mentioned teaching. It surprised me is all." I was explaining this as if I had to. Which I didn't.

Nash just nodded again, and the smirk began to tug at his lips. Asshole.

"I'm leaving now," I said, turning to head back toward the door.

"Any chance her being hired might sway you? Because if that is the case, Coach Rich will want to know. He's already trying to think of ways to sweeten the deal."

"Ezmita is an old friend. I was curious. Jesus, Nash," I replied as my hand hit the door. Just as I opened it and started to walk out, he called, "Good to know. Because she's real nice and fucking gorgeous. If we start working together, I might want to ask her out myself. It's about time I moved on."

I froze for a moment. Anger immediately ignited inside me, and I turned back around to glare at my friend. However, the moment my eyes met his, he threw back his head and howled with laughter. He really was an asshole.

"You made your point. Happy?" I asked.

He was still grinning when he stopped laughing and looked at me. "Oh yeah. Just remembering that face will have me cracking up all damn day."

"Whatever," I replied.

Nash laughed again. "I wish I had a picture. I swear you looked ready to rip the door off the damn hinges. As if I would ask out Ezmita," he replied, shaking his head.

"She's smart and funny and kind, and fucking gorgeous." I was suddenly feeling defensive of her now.

"I remember those things. But a guy never asks out his best friend's one that got away." He paused and then looked away from me. "Just like you'd never ask Tallulah out."

Even now you could still hear the pain in his voice when he said her name. I wanted to argue that his was different. Ezmita had barely been a summer for me. Tallulah had been years for him. But deep down I couldn't because I knew the day I drove out of Lawton and left Ezmita behind, my heart had stayed with her for a long time.

CHAPTER EIGHT

EZMITA

The small garden out back needed work. It had been neglected, as had the little fence around it. I stood there under the shade of the live oak tree that covered a good portion of the backyard. Glancing back over my shoulder, I studied the yellow cottage behind me. It was exactly nine miles from my parents' house. Although it was inside the town limits of Lawton, it was near the border.

There would be no town traffic, and the only neighbors would be the farmers across the street and then the two-story white Colonial across the field. The back door opened and out stepped Mrs. Green, the real estate agent in Lawton who handled most of the rental properties. This house had belonged to Mrs. Mable Potts for over seventy years. She had raised three children in the two-bedroom, thirteen-hundred-square-foot home. It had been well loved.

Although her children were in their sixties now and lived out of state, none of them wanted to part with their childhood home and had decided to rent it out. Now, here I was after taking the job as Lawton High School's new history teacher. I hadn't wanted to go home and tell my parents or my sister. I needed time to prepare my thoughts.

Calling Mrs. Green to show me the rentals that were available had been just to keep me busy, but then she had brought me to this one. It felt like home. This would be my final step at settling down in the place I had once wanted nothing more than to get away from.

"It's eight hundred a month, and that includes your water and garbage pickup only. Electricity, cable, phone, if you want it, will be on you. However, the electricity bill is the highest in July and August at around one eighty. It's out of town a ways, which I think is why it didn't rent out immediately and the fact it's furnished. Most people want to bring their own furniture. But honestly, this is a great price for the house, and the furniture is dated, but I imagine for someone just starting out that would be perfect. It's in good shape and comes with not only the fridge and microwave but the washer and dryer, too. That's rare in a rental house here. Makes up for the fact there is no dishwasher."

"I'll take it," I said.

Mrs. Green beamed brightly. "Wonderful. Mable's children will be pleased to know one of Lawton's new teachers will be living here. Mable taught fourth grade at Lawton Elementary for over fifty years. This will tickle them pink!" she replied, then began pulling out paperwork from her bag.

Within fifteen minutes, I had filled out the paperwork and written a check for the first month's rent along with a deposit. Mrs. Green had handed me two sets of keys to the house that opened both the front and back doors. I had listened while she gave me instructions on the central heating and air, then gave me the electrical company's number to call and have the bill switched over to my name.

There was no regret when I watched her drive away in her red Buick waving her hand out the window and smiling brightly at me while I stood on the front porch. I was making my own decisions, and I was happy about them. I had never truly been happy in Nashville. I had been restless most of the time.

Looking around the small flower beds, which needed some love, a peaceful silence surrounding me, I felt content.

However, I was going to be hungry soon, and there was no food in this house. It was time for a trip to the grocery store, and I needed to face my parents and pack my things before this evening. Tonight, I intended to sleep in my house. Smiling, I went to get the two sets of keys and my purse from the kitchen counter where I had left them.

It had taken less time than I expected to deal with my parents, as they were thrilled I had taken the job in Lawton. My moving into my own place hadn't been that dramatic at all. Papa had even loaded some of the boxes I wanted to go ahead and take tonight into the back of my car. I was inside the grocery part of the Stop and Shop in less than an hour's time.

Momma had gone back to the kitchen to start dinner, Teresa was working at the register on the other side of the shop, where people just came in to pay for gas and not to get groceries. Two newer employees I didn't know were working in the grocery section. I pushed my small cart down the aisles and placed the items I needed inside, feeling more excitement as I thought about my day.

"I heard there's a new history teacher in town." Asa's voice broke into my thoughts, and my head swung from studying the coffee creamer to meet his curious gaze. Even after a day like today, when all had been right in my world, he still managed to affect me. Life couldn't be completely fair, I guess. It would mess up the balance of things.

"You heard correctly," I replied, smiling up at him.

Which was easy enough. Seeing him made me want to smile.

He glanced at my shopping cart, and a small frown creased his forehead. "Didn't know the Shop and Stop did grocery delivery these days," he said when he looked back at me.

Confused it took me a moment to figure out what he was talking about. Then I realized he thought I was working and these items were for someone else. I laughed. "Momma has always done delivery for those who need it. However, that is not what this is," I replied. Feeling a rush of pride, I beamed at my items. "These are my groceries. I not only have a new job in Lawton; I also have my own house," I told him.

His eyes widened at that announcement, and that made me smile even harder. "Your own place, here in Lawton," he repeated as if he was having trouble comprehending it. I knew coming back to this town and making a life was not something he ever wanted to do. He had bigger plans, and I was sure much better offers out there. But I wanted to be here. This was home.

"Lawton is home to me," I told him simply.

He nodded as if he understood, but I knew he didn't. "I'm happy for you, Ezmita."

There was no question that he meant that. The sincerity in his eyes was clear. "Thank you."

He looked like he was going to say something more, possibly a good-bye, but he gave me a crooked grin. "So, where's your new place?"

"It's almost out of town. A small yellow cottage," I told him.

"Mrs. Potts's place. I know it. She was my fourth-grade teacher," he replied then. "That's a great house."

Of course he would know it. He was Asa Griffith; he knew everyone in Lawton, Alabama.

"Yeah, it is," I agreed.

We stood there a moment, and I wondered if I should say more or if there was any more to say. Finally Asa sighed and gave me one last smile. "Well, I guess I need to get what I came in here for and head out before Nash starts calling, asking where I am," Asa said.

I nodded.

"Congratulations on the job and the house," he told me.

"Thank you," I replied, then watched him turn and walk away. There had been so many times over the past five years I had wondered what my life would be like now if I had taken a chance with Asa. Even if I had given a long-distance relationship a chance. Would we have made it? As if the universe was reading my mind, a tall, leggy, gorgeous blonde called out Asa's name and rushed over to him to throw her arms around his neck and began talking to him as if they were the best of friends.

Thanks, Universe. Sometimes a girl just needs reminding.

CHAPTER NINE

ASA

The gang was all here, yet I stood outside on the back porch with a beer in my hand looking into the darkness. I had managed to focus on what was being said inside for almost an hour, and I needed a moment to myself to let my conversation with Ezmita sink in. It wasn't like I hadn't known she had taken the job as a history teacher. Nash had told me earlier today.

For some reason, hearing she'd gotten a house made it seem more final. She was really going to move back here and live. Her life was going to be in Lawton. Which led me to face the fact that Ezmita Ramos living in Lawton did affect my decision. I didn't want it to, but it was going to, and I could feel it.

"Are you hiding or out here thinking about the new history teacher?" Nash asked, and I glanced over my shoulder to see Nash had joined me on the porch. I hadn't even heard him open the back door.

"Neither. Both," I replied.

He laughed and walked over to sit down on one of the chairs beside me. "Hell, at least sit down if you're gonna sit out here and ponder shit," Nash said and waved a hand at the chair beside him.

I decided he was right and sat down beside him.

"Why are you out here?" I asked him. It was his house and his party.

He sighed. "I needed a moment too."

He didn't have to say that being with everyone reminded him of Tallulah. I understood. She had been a part of our group and her not being here now seemed odd. For him it had to be painful. I knew he still loved her, and I was beginning to think he always would.

"She got a house. Ezmita. She got her own place today," I told him.

"Hmm," he replied and took a drink. "Guess she wants to be here."

But did I?

We sat in silence with nothing but the sound of the

occasional car going down the road and the muffled voices and laughter inside the house. Nash had wanted to be here too. This was his home. It was where he wanted to be. He had made that choice.

"Do you regret it?" I asked him, then realized I needed to be clear. He couldn't read my thoughts. "Staying here and not going to Chicago."

Nash turned his head to look at me. "Every damn day," he replied. "Every motherfucking time I take a breath."

I winced. I knew he still loved Tallulah, but I had thought he'd found a way to get on with his life. "It's been a year now. Hasn't it gotten easier?"

Nash took another drink from the bottle in his hand. Then he let out a hard laugh. "No. It hasn't." I thought he was done talking, but then he sighed and looked at me. "I was given a choice. I chose what I thought I wanted. This town, my job, security . . . not once realizing that without her none of this fucking mattered. I chose wrong. Don't do the same thing I did."

Our situations weren't the same, or at least I kept telling myself that. However, I'd had only had that summer with Ezmita but she had stayed with me long after I had left here. "I never wanted to come back here," I said, although Nash already knew this.

"Five years might have gone by quickly, but we all changed. You aren't the same angry kid who left here," he replied as if that answered all my questions.

"You're right. I'm not the same kid who left, so why the hell does the same girl affect me?" I asked him because even though I didn't expect Nash to have my answer he was the only person I felt like I could talk to about it.

He shrugged. "You love her."

I laughed this time. "*Love* is a strong word, my friend."

"Trust me, I know that better than anyone," he replied.

The door behind us slid open. "You two hiding?" Ryker asked as he walked out onto the porch.

"We were. You fucking found us, though," Nash replied dryly. Although the two were cousins, they had always seemed like brothers to me. I think we all viewed them that way.

Ryker walked over to the railing and leaned against it to face the two of us. "This about the coaching position or the new history teacher?" Ryker asked.

I sighed and rolled my eyes. Did everyone in this town know my business?

"Both. They're one and the same these days," Nash told him.

I shot him an accusatory glare. He shrugged. "What? Don't look at me. This is Lawton. Folks talk. Hell, I would bet every neighbor I got is discussing the new history teacher over dinner tonight or wondering if you'll take the coaching position or not."

I ran my hand through my short hair and groaned. This was why I hated small towns. The gossip. There was never any privacy. Unless your father was beating the shit out of your mother. Somehow he could get away with that and no one would figure it out. The reminder put a sour taste in my mouth, and I stood up. "One of the many reasons I wanted out of this place," I said.

"It's got just as many pros as it does cons. Maybe more. Hell, we added a pro today. History teacher is smoking hot," Nash drawled. I knew he was saying it just to rile me, but I still scowled at him.

Nash started laughing and took a drink. "Go on and take that job in Georgia. Leave Ezmita Ramos here in Lawton. I might not make a move, but someone will. Next thing you know you'll come to visit and she'll be married with a kid. Sleep on that, why don't ya."

"Jesus, Nash," Ryker muttered. "You're fucking harsh."

I wanted to ignore the image in my head, but thanks to Nash it was there. It wasn't going away, either. Damn him and his meddling. He wanted me in Lawton for his sake, and I knew that. However, he was right. One day Ezmita would get married. She would have a family.

Was I ready to see that? Would I ever be?

CHAPTER TEN

EZMITA

I had spent the past two days cleaning house, moving in, and shopping at the local consignment stores for things to make this place look like mine. Now, I stood in the living room. The pretty teal afghan I had bought thrown over the faded tan sofa brightened it up. Pictures of my family and me with my friends back in Nashville sat on the mantel. A large slightly faded and overstuffed red chair now had a brightly colored throw pillow on it. I had moved it to the left of the sofa and turned it slightly so it was facing the fireplace.

I had made it mine, and I loved it. Wrapping my arms around my waist, I spun in a circle to take it all in. Sure, there was more I needed to buy once I could afford it, but for now I had all I truly required.

A knock on the front door interrupted my happy moment, and I hoped my momma hadn't decided to bring those awful throw pillows she had tried to make me take yesterday. Walking to the door, I began preparing my speech as to why they wouldn't work with my décor. There was a good chance she would force me to take them and I would have to keep them in the closet and only pull them out when she was visiting.

I took a quick peek out the window to the right of the door and when my eyes found the back of Asa Griffith's tall, muscular build I froze. That was the very last person I had expected it to be. Letting the curtain fall back into place before he turned and caught me looking at him, I took a deep, calming breath and then went to straighten my hair when I realized it was in a bun. The same bun I had slept in last night. Groaning, I glanced down at my dirty work clothing and wanted to cry. The cutoff jeans and once-pink tank top were old, and I had dirt, dust, and, I was just noticing, some cookie batter across my boobs.

Another knock on the door, and I sighed. It didn't matter what I looked like. It was Asa. He didn't care. I was no longer the young girl trying to get his attention. I was an independent woman who didn't need the appreciation of a man to feel good about myself. With that mini pep talk, I opened the door and put a smile on my face.

"Hello," I said in greeting.

Asa's grin made my stomach flutter, and I felt like in that moment my stomach was a traitor to the rest of my body. "Hey, I hope I'm not interrupting anything," he replied.

I glanced down at myself. "Nope. Although it looks like I could use a shower. I've been cleaning most of the day."

"Need any help?" he asked.

My cheeks heated because I knew he meant cleaning, but still it put other images in my head and I wished they would go away.

"With the moving, that is. I assume you can handle the shower on your own."

A nervous laugh bubbled out of me, and his grin broke into one of those big smiles that made my knees weak. Damn, my knees were traitors now.

"I, uh, no thanks. I think it's all done," I replied, then stepped back from the door. "You can come in if you would like." Why was I inviting him inside? What was I doing?

Asa stepped into my house, and it looked even smaller with him in it. "Smells like cookies," he said, looking around.

"I just took a batch out of the oven a few minutes ago," I told him. "Chocolate chip," I added, then thought about the batter on my tank top.

"Those are my favorite," he said, his gaze on me instead of the house.

I didn't doubt it. Asa liked sweets. "Follow me," I replied, unable to keep the grin off my face. For a moment, it was as if five years hadn't happened and things were just as we'd left them. But only for a moment.

I walked into the kitchen and placed three cookies on a plate, then took a glass from the cabinet and poured a glass of milk. When I turned back to him, Asa was watching me. "Here you go," I said, handing the cookies and milk to him. "Have a seat." I waved my hand at the table behind him and then went to pull out a chair and sit down.

"Thanks. I didn't know I would be getting cookies when I came to see you. I should have come sooner," he told me, then winked. It was just a wink. Guys had winked at me before. It wasn't something exclusive to Asa. However, the way my entire body responded to his winking at me was the issue.

Why? Why did he have to look like this? Why did I have to feel things for him? Why? It was so unfair. I hadn't regretted my decision five years ago. Not one time, until this week. Now I kept wondering, what if I had followed him to Mississippi? What if we had stayed together? What if? Ugh, that would never have happened. He was gorgeous, for starters, and the girls would have been all over him.

"When did you decide to become a teacher?" he asked me.

I snapped out of my inner debate, grateful for the distraction. My thoughts had become a dangerous place. "My second year of college," I told him. "What about you? What did you major in?"

His smirk as he chewed up the bite of cookie in his mouth was intriguing. I had wondered more than once what it was he had chosen to do with his life since hearing he hadn't gone into the NFL draft like everyone thought he would.

"Spanish," he replied, then took a drink of milk.

"Spanish?" I repeated, knowing I heard him correctly but trying to process it. Why would he major in Spanish?

He nodded. "Yeah. Spanish. I want to teach it along with coaching high school football."

He was going to teach Spanish. I laughed then.

"Is that funny?" he asked me, his grin tugging at his lips.

I shrugged. "Yes but I don't know why. I guess I wasn't expecting you to tell me Spanish. I was thinking a business degree or something to do with sports medicine."

"I wanted to be a teacher," he replied. "I was good at Spanish, and I enjoyed it."

It had been his mother's first language. I wanted to ask him how often she had spoken it at home, but I didn't know if talking about her upset him. I didn't know much about Asa anymore. My smile faded.

"You'll have the attention of all the female students," I told him, keeping it light.

He finished off his last cookie and leaned back in his hair. "You think so?" he asked, studying me.

It was my time to smirk. "I hope you don't have a jealous girlfriend," I blurted out without thinking. Dang it. Why did I have to say anything about a girlfriend?

He shook his head. "No, I don't have one of those."

I had dug this hole, and apparently I was going to keep digging. "That's good she's not jealous. A jealous female can be difficult."

He chuckled, then leaned forward, resting his elbows on the table as he looked at me. "Is this your way of asking if I have a girlfriend?"

Yes, no, maybe. I shrugged. "I was just making small talk," I replied nervously.

"Okay," he replied after a few moments. "Can I have a tour of the house?"

He wasn't going to tell me. Which meant he did in fact have a girlfriend. Right? I didn't care. He would be gone soon. I needed to remember that. I didn't need to know about his life.

"Sure," I replied, standing up. "It's a short tour, though."

He stood up then, and we were close. Too close. My body wasn't ready for this kind of close. Not with him, at least. The sooner Asa left Lawton, the better.

"I don't," he said, not stepping back and putting much-needed space between us. He was so big now, and being so close to his massive, muscular body made me tingle in places I should not be tingling.

As always, I had to tilt my head back to look up at him. He was studying me for a reaction to his two words. I wasn't sure what he had been talking about because my heart had begun to beat faster as my mind went to other things being this close to him. "Um . . . what?" I asked, jerking my gaze from his and forcing myself to move a few steps ahead of him.

"A girlfriend. I don't have one of those," he replied.

Unable to help myself, I smiled.

CHAPTER ELEVEN

ASA

Walking out of the front door of Lawton High School, I saw Nash headed in my direction. He was grinning. How the hell did he know already? I had just walked out of the meeting with Ms. Campbell. There was no possible way he knew.

"Welcome home," he said when he reached me.

I glanced back at the door as it closed. "How the hell?" I asked him.

"Ms. Campbell texted Rich the moment you took the position," he replied. "The old man was beaming, he was so damn happy. I swear he let out a fucking hoot and punched his fist into the air."

It felt right. All of it. Nash was right. No matter what had happened with my dad, Lawton was home. That field at the bottom of the hill was home. I belonged here.

"I don't even care that you took it for a woman. I'm just glad you took it," he said and slapped my back.

"You think I took the job because of Ezmita?" I asked him.

"I know you did," he shot back at me, then laughed. "The moment you found out she was going to be teaching here, it was in your eyes. You were coming home."

I started to argue but stopped. He was right. There was no use denying it. I had tried life without her in it, and I didn't like it.

A familiar truck pulled up behind Nash and after it a Tahoe I also recognized. "Did you call everyone?" I asked him.

"Nah, I just sent a text to the ones that mattered," he replied.

West climbed out of the truck, followed by Ryker and Brady in the Tahoe. A Range Rover then came pulling in too fast and slammed on the brakes. The driver door swung open, and Gunner climbed out grinning like the cocky son of a bitch he was. They were all here.

"I got the beer," Gunner said and reached inside his Range Rover to pull out a six-pack. "Ready?"

"When did you get in town?" I asked him.

"About thirty minutes ago," he replied. "Then you had to go and steal the damn show."

We all began walking down the hill toward the field house.

"So I hear you said yes because of a girl," Gunner said.

"Of course he did," West replied for me. "His ass could be anywhere. He came back to Lawton."

"Nothing wrong with that," Nash told him.

"Didn't say there was, but Asa has reasons to hate this place. More so than I do," Gunner said.

He was right. I did have reasons to hate Lawton. Memories that would always be attached to this town. But I had more good memories than I had bad. "That field is where I grew up, where I made some of the best memories of my life," I reminded all of them. It was true for them as much as it was me. "If I'm going to coach the game I love, then why do it on a field that means nothing to me when I can do it on the field that made me?"

Ryker grinned and shook his head. "Damn. Now you got me getting all sentimental. Hand me a beer, Gunner."

Coach Rich walked out of the locker room to find us sitting in the middle of the field drinking beer. "I should've expected to see the whole lot of you. Just clean that shit up when you're done, and Asa, welcome home, son," he called out before walking toward his truck.

"Where you gonna live?" Brady asked me.

"With me," Nash replied before I could.

I shrugged and took a drink. "I guess with Nash for now. Haven't thought that far."

"He ain't thought about nothing but Ezmita Ramos since getting back in town," Ryker said.

I couldn't argue with him. He was right; I had thought of little else.

CHAPTER TWELVE

EZMITA

My sister's graduation was in two hours, and since I had spent another day working in the house, I was just getting out of the shower when the doorbell rang. I quickly wrapped my hair in a towel and pulled on a T-shirt dress that covered enough of my body before rushing to the door. The electrician said he would be here tomorrow between nine and twelve to fix the two outlets that weren't working. Unless he was a day early, then I wasn't expecting anyone.

I didn't stop to check out the window and opened the door.

Once again, there stood Asa surprising me with his presence. I paused, leaving the screen door closed between us. His coming around like this was going to make it harder when he left town again. As much as I enjoyed seeing him standing on my front porch, I also didn't want that memory haunting me once he was gone. I had already mourned the loss of Asa in my life. I didn't want to go through that another time.

"Asa." I said his name, unsure if it was a greeting or a question.

"Looks like you're getting ready for something," he said, taking in my appearance.

"Lawton graduation," I told him.

"Ah yes, I forgot about that. I didn't get a Lawton graduation. Covid stopped that," he replied. "I . . ." His shoulders lifted and fell with a sigh. "Look, I know you're busy and I should leave you alone to get ready, but I don't think I can. I need to talk to you."

I reached out and opened the screen door for him. When he took it from me, I stepped back and let him come inside. He was right that I needed to get ready, but this was also Asa telling me he needed to talk to me. I had an Asa weakness that hadn't gone away over time. I was accepting that now, just as I needed to accept this was fleeting. He was leaving.

Asa didn't walk very far into my house. He stopped just inside, and the smell of his cologne was so dang sexy I wished he had stayed outside. Now my house was going to smell like him.

"I took the Spanish teacher position and offensive coordinator coaching position at Lawton today," he said, turning to face me.

Of all the things I'd expected him to say, this was not one of them. "Oh" was what came out of my mouth as a response.

He smirked then. "Yeah, 'oh,'" he echoed.

I shook my head and smiled. "I'm sorry. You just surprised me. I didn't know you were interviewing for a job at Lawton. I thought this was the last place you wanted to be."

He gave a short laugh and ran a hand through his hair. The way his bicep flexed as he did the small movement caught my attention. He wasn't leaving. I would see him every day at work. This was slowly sinking in, and so was my panic.

"I didn't intend to take the Lawton job, until . . . well, until you decided to stay in town. I thought I wanted to work at the larger high school offering me a position in Georgia. I could say I'm surprised by my decision, but the truth is I'm not," he said.

I stood there staring at him at a loss for words. I wasn't sure what my words should be, because the truth was not something I could speak right now or ever.

"Hell, it's been five years. One would think my seeing you again wouldn't affect me. That I would have been over you by now. I thought I was. Then I saw you and nothing had changed. The way you make me feel. My inability to think of anything other than you. My need to be near you. It's all still right fucking there. I am connected to that football field, and coaching kids on it will mean something to me. But that is not why I took this job. I want to be here because I want that chance now. The one we were too young to take. I want to prove to you I'm not that kid anymore that you can't trust. The one whose life had screwed him up." He took a step toward me, and his hand reached out and brushed mine.

"My last words to you five years ago were 'You'll always be the one.' I didn't know then how true they were. But they are. I hadn't wanted to say good-bye to you because it sounded so fucking final. I couldn't do it. Deep down I knew then one day I would get that chance. I needed to run from this place and the pain here. You needed to chase your dreams and go your way. But we are both back. We did those things, and we are back where it all began. You don't have to say anything today. I just needed to tell you." He stepped back again, and then I watched as he turned to leave.

He was leaving? After all that? I hadn't even had a

chance to say anything. Although I had needed a moment to get my thoughts together and accept that this was real. It was happening. I wasn't daydreaming.

"Yes," I blurted out. "I want that." I said the words while his back was turned for fear I would lose the nerve when he looked at me again.

He turned back around, and the smile on his face made his eyes twinkle. I was expecting him to respond, but he took three long strides toward me, then his massive hands cupped my face just as he lowered his head. "You might be a little late to graduation," he whispered, then his lips touched mine and the world faded away.

The boy I had loved from afar for years, and then witnessed his darkest moment and fallen in love with, had never left my heart. I knew loving the man he had become would be too easy. Life has a funny way of coming full circle even when you are determined to go another path. I was thankful for fate. Because fate had brought me home. To Lawton, to my family, and to the man I was meant to love.

NASH AND TALLULAH

"Even after you destroyed me, all I wanted was you. Why can't I get over you?"

CHAPTER ONE

NASH

Most of the time, I kept myself busy. It helped distract me. Problem was I needed fucking distracting every damn day. This should have gotten easier. Isn't there a point when someone heals from heartbreak? When would I stop loving Tallulah? It was fucking time. I had suffered long enough.

I knew once everyone was back in town it was going to be an adjustment. Once again, life after Tallulah screwing with me. She had become a part of us. Everything in my life she had fit into so perfectly. One year wasn't enough time to get over that, I guess. At least not for me.

Asa moved in to my biggest guest bedroom yesterday. Gunner and Willa were taking the other guest bedroom while they were in town. Seeing them together wasn't easy, but seeing any happy couple was hard. It reminded me of all I had lost.

The back door opened, and Asa stepped out with a cup of coffee in his hand.

"Slept late," I said, raising my eyebrows.

He grinned, then shrugged. "Five years, man. Five fucking long years. We had some catching up to do."

I didn't need the details on what that catching up entailed. My sex life was nonexistent. "I'm surprised you came back last night."

He shrugged. "I'd have stayed, but I don't want to rush her. I came back, made a life decision based on her, and then went and bluntly told her she was it for me. Then we . . ." He paused and cut his eyes in my direction. "Uh, well, you know."

Yeah, I knew. I nodded.

A car door slammed, and we both turned our heads to see Ryker coming around the corner of the house. He looked like a man on a mission. I could see the tension in his shoulders, and I braced myself. Something was up.

Ryker took the steps up to the back porch two at a time. When he got to the top, he stopped and looked at me shoving his hands in the pockets of his jeans, then sighed heavily. "She's here, man. She's in fucking Lawton."

I didn't have to ask him who. There was only one "she" that would affect me. I tried to act as if I didn't care when my chest felt like it was being twisted inside. With a shrug, I picked up my bottle of water and took a drink. "Her mom lives here," I replied.

I didn't miss the concerned look between Asa and Ryker. They both knew how I felt about Tallulah. Asa didn't know the details of the breakup, but Ryker did. I'd lost my damn mind there for a while. Ryker had been the one to pull me back when I tried like hell to destroy myself. Without him, I'd have probably lost my damn job or ended up in jail, or worse, I'd be dead.

"Who told you?" I asked him, wishing I didn't care.

"West called me. Maggie ran into her this morning at the Drip," he said.

The Drip was a new coffee place in town with fancy shit. Figures she'd go there. She likes her fancy coffee. The kitchen counter had once been covered with all her coffee supplies. It took her so damn long to make one cup of coffee with all that crap. I'd teased her about leaving no room for anything else. Complained that my Keurig was being shoved in the corner. And now I'd give anything in this fucking world for it to all be back in there, her standing in her baggy cut-off sweatpants and fuzzy socks.

I took another drink of water. My chest felt so damn

constricted, breathing was hard. I hated remembering, but then again it was all I had of her. Memories.

"She didn't get an invite to the field dedication," Ryker told me. "I swear."

Yeah, she had. I had sent her one. I hadn't thought she would come, but that lost part of me that missed her had hoped she would. Believing that she felt nothing for me anymore seemed so fucking impossible when she still owned me. I woke up with her on my mind and went to bed at night wishing she was in my arms.

"I know she and Aurora keep in touch, but trust me, man, she wouldn't have invited her. She knows what you went through," Ryker assured me.

"I know she didn't," I said, then stood up and looked at him. "I did."

Ryker said nothing as he stood there, but I could see the pain in his eyes. He was worried about me. Worried seeing her was going to set me off again. We had this new venture, and the football camps started in a couple weeks. There was no time for me to fall apart again.

"The field was hers, too. Just like it was ours. We all have memories there. We all should be there for the dedication. Even her," I told him, then turned and walked inside the house. I didn't need to be around anyone right now, and I sure as hell didn't want to hear how it was a mistake to invite her.

It was my decision, and if it was a mistake, that was mine too. I'd made enough mistakes already. What was one more? I had already lost her. It couldn't get worse than that. Nothing could, and I knew nothing ever would.

CHAPTER TWO

TALLULAH

"I made brownies," Mom said as I walked into the house.

"It's a little early for brownies, isn't it?" I asked her.

She beamed at me. "It's never a bad time for brownies. Especially when my girl is back home for a visit. I swear you don't look like you eat anymore. Doesn't Chicago have the world's best pizza, or is it hot dogs?"

I sank down onto the bright yellow sofa with hot pink and blue throw pillows. I was glad my mom's new husband embraced her creative, over-the-top decorating. Some men wouldn't be able to deal with the crazy colors and artistic painted murals all over the walls. Being back here felt good. I needed to see my mom, and I realized I needed to be home.

"It's both," I told her. "They are proud of both their pizza and their hot dogs, but I don't eat either."

She cocked her head to the side. "Maybe if you did you wouldn't be so thin. I understand your wanting to eat healthy, but there is a point when you get too thin, and sweetie, you have found it. Now come eat a brownie or five."

I patted the cushion beside me. "I will later. I'm not real hungry right now. Come sit with me," I told her.

Mom walked across the living room and sat down beside me. I immediately laid my head on her shoulder. Home. My soul needed home. Or maybe it just needed my mom.

"Oh, honey, did you see him when you were out?" she asked, moving so that her arm was wrapped around me.

I shook my head. No, if I had seen Nash, there was a good chance I'd be in tears right now. "I saw Maggie," I told her.

"That's West's girlfriend, right?"

I nodded.

She squeezed me. "You're gonna see them all soon. I know it's hard."

They would all be together. I'd have to see Nash with someone else. Some other woman would be there beside him. He'd have his arm around her. I felt the sick knot in my stomach remind me of all I had lost.

"I told myself it was time I come back and face it all. Nash sent the invitation. The writing on the envelope was his. He wanted me here, and even after all that happened, I couldn't not come. But, Mom, I don't know if I can do it. See him and not shatter. What if he's with someone else now? How do I stand there and look at that?"

Mom sighed deeply and patted me. "It won't be easy. It might be the hardest thing you've ever done. But what if he's not with someone else? What if he wants to see you too?"

I closed my eyes tightly and fought back the tears. She didn't see his face when he'd walked into my office to surprise me and found Charles there with me. He had looked so broken. The look on his face still haunted me. If he had just given me a chance to explain . . . but he hadn't trusted me enough. His jealousy had been getting worse, and in the end it destroyed us.

"I keep thinking one day it will get easier. One day I will wake up and not miss him. One day I will be able to make it through the day without thinking about him. It's been over a year now, and that day hasn't come."

Mom kissed my head. "I'm sorry, baby. It hurts my heart to know you are hurting. I wish I had the words to make it all better, but even Momma can't heal your heart. It just takes time. The harder you loved, the longer it takes."

That wasn't what I wanted to hear, because there was a good chance it would take forever.

We sat there in silence while Mom gently ran her fingers through my hair. When I was a kid, there wasn't anything that Mom couldn't make better with brownies and cuddling me. Life gets bigger than that the older you get. I wish I could go back to the time she had the power to fix it all for me.

"I was thinking about turning the guest bathroom into the Gryffindor common room," Mom told me. Which meant she was going to paint the walls and ceiling to look like the Gryffindor common room. Several parts of the house had Harry Potter paintings.

"Have you grown tired of Alice in Wonderland?" I asked. "I'm fond of the Cheshire cat and the Mad Hatter." Which was what that bathroom was currently painted with.

"I think it's time for a change," she replied. "Want to help me?"

I lifted my head to look at her. "You want to do it now? Today?"

She shrugged. "Why not? Painting always makes me feel better."

"I thought baking made you feel better."

"It does, but you don't eat enough for all the baking that would require. Let's paint instead," she replied with a grin.

"Sounds like a good plan," I replied. I had nothing else to do. My friends in this town were Nash's friends first, which meant I'd lost them too. Why had I wanted to come back here so badly? Why did the idea of going back to Chicago make me want to cry? All I had here was Mom. I had nothing else. Yet now that I was here, I didn't want to think about going back to my life in Chicago.

"First you must eat a brownie," Mom said, standing up. "Then we will paint."

Giving in so that she would stop worrying about my weight, I stood up to follow her to the kitchen when a knock on the front door stopped me. Mom paused and turned around. "Wonder who that is," she said, frowning. I didn't move as she walked past me and headed to answer the door. Although I was closer to the door, I didn't make a move to get it. No one in this town would be coming to see me.

"Riley." My mother sounded as surprised as I felt.

Why was Riley Young here? We hadn't spoken since the breakup. Mom moved and waved her inside. "Come on in. I just made brownies, and we were about to have one. Please come join us."

Riley's eyes met mine, and a small smile touched her lips. "Hey," she said almost cautiously.

"Hey," I replied, not sure what else to say or why she was here. The last time we had spoken, Brady had graduated from the University of Alabama with a degree in architecture. He'd already had interviews in Nashville. I didn't know if he'd gotten a job there or if he was here now. They had done the long-distance thing successfully for four years. Riley had done college online and stayed in Lawton to raise her daughter. I was glad they'd made it.

"Maggie told me she saw you this morning. I didn't know you were in town," she explained. "I wanted to stop by and catch up, if . . . if that's okay."

I nodded, willing myself not to cry. "Yeah, I'd like that."

"And I'll leave you both to do just that," Mom said, beaming brightly, then left the room without mentioning the brownies again.

I motioned toward the chairs across from the sofa. "Uh, have a seat," I told her, feeling awkward. Once we had been close. Riley had been the closest female friend I'd ever had. I missed her, and I missed Bryony, too.

She reached up to tuck some hair behind her ear as she sat and I saw it then. The diamond on her hand. The sunlight through the windows hit it just right, and it sparkled beautifully. "You're engaged," I said.

Riley nodded her head. "Yeah," she said.

"When?" I asked, realizing just how much I had missed.

"Bryony's seventh birthday party," she replied with a soft smile on her face.

"Congratulations. I mean, we all knew this day was coming, but still, I'm happy for all three of you," I told her honestly. "Did Brady get a job in Nashville?" I asked.

"Yes, the company is in Nashville, but he is working in Cullman. It's for a new shopping development. We bought a house in Lawton." She laughed then. "Who would have thought six years ago that I'd have wanted to buy a house and raise Bryony here? But it's home now. It's where we belong."

"I'm happy for you, I really am," I told her.

A slight frown touched her lips then. "What about you? How is Chicago? Are you still loving it there?"

I wasn't sure I had ever loved it there. I shrugged. "I don't know what I'm doing, honestly. Do I love Chicago? No. But is this my home still? I don't know. I can't figure out where I fit and what I'm supposed to do." I said more than I meant to. Riley hadn't stopped by for me to unload on her.

"He's lost too. He's got his job, and that's all he does."

"He" was Nash. I didn't have to ask.

"But he's happy with his job?"

She nodded. "Yes."

"And he's got the youth football camp starting up," I added.

She nodded again. "Yeah, he does, but that doesn't make him any less lost. It just keeps him busy."

I ran a hand through my hair and turned my gaze to the window. "He sent me the invitation. He didn't sign it or anything, but I recognized his handwriting on the envelope. He wanted me to come. But now that I'm here, I'm scared it was the wrong thing."

"Why?" she asked, her voice soft, almost a whisper.

Turning back to her, I felt a lump form in my throat. "Because seeing him again may crush me."

Riley leaned toward me with a serious expression. "I don't know exactly what happened. No one does except possibly Ryder. But Brady says Nash doesn't talk. What little we all know is what Ryder told us, and that's not a lot. I won't lie: at first I was so mad at you. I was sure I hated you for hurting Nash that way." She paused. "For hurting all of us. But as time went on, the more I thought about it, the harder it was for me to believe that you had cheated on Nash. It just didn't sound like you. I've wanted to call you and talk to you, and I swear I have picked up the phone to text you a million times and stopped myself because I didn't know what to say. But when Maggie said you were in town I knew I had to come talk to you. I had to see you. Not because of Nash but because you were my friend. One I miss terribly."

I reached up and wiped a tear that had escaped and rolled down my face. I already knew what they all thought of me here. She may not have texted me, but I had received an angry text from Ryder. I never responded to it, but I had kept it.

"I didn't cheat," I said. "I would never have cheated on Nash. I loved him." I stopped before I broke down and started really crying.

"Can you tell me what happened?" she asked me. I knew it wasn't because she was being nosy. She had been hurt by all this too. She wanted to understand.

"Charles was my supervisor when I first got the job. He was helpful and nice. I appreciated how easy he made things for me just beginning. The models that the firm hired for marketing always seemed to end up in his bed. It was a joke around the office. He was a friend, and that was all. I realize now I was naive. I didn't notice things changing for him. I didn't see him as more than a friend and colleague. The first clue was when he brought me flowers he had picked up on the way to work. Then I finally noticed it had been a while since he'd come to work bragging about his latest model conquest. He had even stopped going to the photo shoots. I began to grow concerned by the attention I was getting from him. He was giving me bigger and more important jobs. Ones that I didn't deserve. There were others there that should be getting those jobs. They'd been there for years waiting for chances like I was being handed." I stopped and took a deep breath. Remembering this was hard to do. My mistakes had cost me Nash.

"After overhearing two of the women in my office whispering about me and saying I had to be sleeping with Charles, I knew I had to talk to him about it. Stop it. I asked him if he could come to my office before he left that afternoon, and he did. I told him what I heard and how I thought they were right to be upset and angry. I didn't want him to give me any more jobs that others should be getting a chance at. Then . . . then he told me he had fallen in love with me. He went on and on telling me how I was all he could think about. He thought we were perfect for each other. I immediately told him I was in love with Nash and that was not going to happen. He grabbed me then and kissed me. I was shocked. I didn't expect that. But more than that, I didn't expect Nash to come walking in on it. When I shoved Charles away from me, it was then I saw Nash standing there in the doorway. He had flowers." My voice cracked, and I dropped my head into my hands. "He had flowers," I repeated on a sob. "And then he left. He just turned and walked away. I ran after him, and . . . and when he finally stopped and looked at me, he told me to shut up. He didn't want to hear my lies. He didn't want to see my face again. Then he threw my flowers on the floor at my feet and called me a bitch. I . . . I couldn't speak. Words wouldn't come. It felt as if my soul had been ripped from my body. I just stood there."

Riley blew out a breath. "Wow," she said.

I just nodded and wiped at the tears staining my face.

"And Charles?" she asked hesitantly.

"He was fired. I went to resign, and when my boss asked why, I told her. She wouldn't allow me to resign, and the next day Charles was gone."

"Nash never let you tell him all this?" she asked.

I shook my head. "No. He had already been acting strange. I knew he was jealous of Charles. I'd told him about Charles. I didn't keep secrets. Every time Nash came to Chicago, Charles made it a point to drop by my office and say hello. I think he knew Nash was jealous of his being around me. He played off that. I was so damn blind."

Riley stood up and moved over to sit beside me on the sofa. She reached for my hand and held it firmly in both of hers. "You're kind and have a big heart. That was taken advantage of by an asshole."

I sniffled. It didn't make this better. I had still lost Nash. My heart was still damaged beyond repair.

CHAPTER THREE

NASH

It looked like a training facility. Two football fields, four field houses, stadium lighting, and equipment lined up ready to be used. Yet I could still see the field that it had been. The one with the bonfire, the trucks, the old tires and logs brought out for seating, and the keg that sat in the middle of it all. So many memories were on this land, some of the best and the worst. We had all grown up together out there, and now it was over. We were no longer kids but adults with different lives.

"We did it," Ryker said coming to stand beside me. "Hunter would be so fucking proud of this."

Hunter. The only one of us that would forever be a

teenage boy in our heads. He wouldn't grow old and age like the rest of us. The hate crime that had gotten him shot as he had stood to defend Ryker made him a hero that died tragically. My gaze moved to the stone memorial with his name that sat in the spot where he'd taken his last breath. It was there to remind us all of the boy who was a part of us but didn't get to stay.

"I'm glad Aurora is going to speak. Hunter would want her to be the one to unveil the memorial and talk about him," I said.

"She's nervous, but she wants to do it. She still worries about how her voice sounds, even though I tell her daily how fucking beautiful it is." Ryker sighed. Although she had the hearing implant she still heard things differently. Including her own voice. "Her parents are all going to be here, and she wants to do it for her mom and dad enough that she will overcome her nerves."

I nodded but said nothing. We stood there awhile, staring out over what we had spent the last year working toward. I had thought it would bring me some kind of joy. Some happiness even. But the hole in my chest made that impossible.

"When are you going to talk to her? You sent her the invitation. She came. Now follow through," Ryker said.

I had fought with myself all damn day about going over

to her mom's house. I just hadn't been able to do it for fear that seeing her would be more than I could take. I felt like I was on a ledge and I was holding on the best I could. Tallulah was the only one I feared could push me off the damn ledge. She was the reason I struggled to hold on in the first place.

"I talked to Brady. Riley went to see her," Ryker said.

"They were close once," I reminded him.

"Which is why you need to go see Tallulah. She talked to Riley, and Brady said you needed to talk to her too."

I gripped the railing in front of me and glared out straight ahead. They didn't understand. They had no fucking idea how hard that would be. Neither of them had faced the pain I'd been through this past year. "I can't," I bit out through my clenched teeth.

"Then why did you invite her? And don't give me that *we all belong here* shit. That's not why you did it."

"Too many shots of Patrón," I replied.

"You can blame it on the damn tequila all you want, but we both know you sent it because you wanted to see her. You miss her. You aren't the same person without her. If there is a chance that you could fix this, that you could have her back, then don't waste it. You walked away last time and didn't give her a chance to explain. It's been a year. It's time now. It's fucking past time."

I shoved away from the railing and ran my hands through my hair as a growl of frustration rose in my chest. "ALL I CAN SEE IS HER FUCKING LIPS ON HIS!" I yelled and kicked the wall, then slammed both my palms flat against it as the image replayed in my head. Taunting me like it always did. "I can't see anything else," I choked out then and laid my forehead on the cool bricks. "Daily it rips me apart, but then I miss her so damn much, I think I can forget it. If she'd just come back to me," I admitted.

Ryker let out a heavy sigh. "I can't make you talk to her. No one can. That's gotta be you, brother. She came for you. Not this field or anyone else. She came for you. Now the ball is in your field."

I didn't say anything. I stayed there with my forehead against the damn wall and my eyes closed. Ryker walked away, leaving me to my own demons. He had said what he'd come to say, and I knew he was right. I just didn't know if I was strong enough to look at her.

Needing a distraction, I went to my truck and headed to the only bar in town, Lions Turf. It was owned by a former Lawton Lion running back who had played with my dad and uncle. I'd stay away from the tequila tonight and stick with whiskey. While stopped at a red light, I sent out a text to the guys, even Ryker, who I knew would be pissed this was where I'd ended up instead of Tallulah's. By the time I pulled into the parking lot, West and Gunner were already stepping out of Gunner's expensive wheels.

"I'm guessing you talked to Brady," Gunner called out when I got out of my truck.

"Not here to talk about her. Just want to drink and play some pool," I warned him. Gunner had no filter, nor did he fucking want one. He said whatever he was thinking.

We were almost at the door when Brady pulled up in the parking lot. He was still several feet away when Gunner yelled, "He don't want to talk about Tallulah, so don't bring that shit up."

I turned and shoved open the door, wishing I'd just come here by myself.

"Jesus, Gunner," West muttered.

"What? I was shutting it down," Gunner replied.

I headed for the bar. It was past time I had a drink.

"Ryker coming?" Gunner asked then.

I shrugged. "Not sure."

"What about Asa?" Gunner asked.

I didn't reply.

"He's probably banging it out with Ezmita. He waited five years for her. We might not see him for a while," West replied.

I wasn't in the mood to discuss anyone's sex life, and I hoped those two would shut the hell up or at least let me get enough drinks in me first.

"I stand corrected!" West announced.

Glancing back over my shoulder, I saw Asa and Ryker walking in behind Brady. They all came. Every fucking one.

CHAPTER FOUR

TALLULAH

This was harder than I had anticipated. When Riley had called me this evening and asked me to come to her house for a girls' night, I'd said yes because I didn't feel like I could tell her no. Now that I was here surrounded by the females that had once been a big part of my life, I wasn't sure my emotions could take this. I didn't know what Riley had told them, but the moment I had walked in the door, Willa had run over and thrown her arms around me. Aurora had smiled at me and said she had missed me. Then Maggie had walked up to me and handed me a glass of bubbly pink wine with a grin on her face.

"Tallulah, you remember Ezmita," Riley said as she

brought a tray of cookies over to set on the coffee table.

"Yes, it's good to see you. Are you and Asa . . ." I paused, unsure if that was why she was here. The last time she had been around the group had been the summer after graduation.

She blushed, then nodded.

"Finally," Maggie said, picking up a cookie from the tray. "Asa admitted his feelings and did something about it."

"Speaking of relationships and all," Willa said, "I'm just going to grab the elephant in the room by the trunk and get that over with. Don't be mad at Riley, but she told us what happened. I wasn't surprised. I'd already figured it was something like that. You're not a cheater. So that's all clear, and you're here just like old times."

Riley looked at me nervously, and I smiled. I wasn't upset she'd told them. It wasn't a secret; it was just hard to talk about.

"Ryker is trying to get him to talk to you," Aurora said softly.

I nodded my head but said nothing.

"All right, enough of that," Riley said. "Let's drink and"—she glanced at the bag in my right hand—"eat whatever Tallulah's momma has sent in that bag."

Laughing, I walked over and put the large white bag on the table beside the cookies. Mom had been so excited that

I was going she'd packaged up all the brownies, then put them, along with the lemon bars she'd made this afternoon and all the fudge she had stored in the freezer, in a bag for me to bring. "She can't help herself," I said. "Baking and painting are her two passions in life."

"Oh my God!" Maggie squealed when she pulled out the plastic container with the fudge in it. "I'm going to gain ten pounds tonight."

The eating, drinking, and talking began, and before I knew it two hours had gone by. There was little I didn't know about everyone now. I'd been caught up on it all. I wished I knew what I was going to do next. I seemed to be the only one lost. Which made my world even more lonely.

"Oh no," Maggie blurted out in the middle of Riley telling a story about Bryony. We all looked her way as she jumped up and hurried to the window. "One, two, three," she whispered, then turned around to face us. Except her gaze wasn't on the group, it was on me. "It's the guys. All of them."

My heart began to beat faster as her words sunk in. I stared at her, unsure what I should do and hoping someone would instruct me. Did I stay? Did I leave out the back door? Was I overreacting?

"Brady is smarter than this," Riley said, standing up and going to the door.

"Unfortunately Gunner isn't. He likes to stir things up," Willa said, frowning.

"I'll go out there and stop them," Maggie offered.

"No," I said, holding up a hand. "No. It's fine. Really. He must know I'm here. I did come because he sent the invitation. We were going to see each other anyway." My voice sounded calm, and I was relieved it didn't give away the current state of my emotions.

"This might be a good thing," Aurora said, and I knew she was trying to ease my worries. I doubted anything good would come of it.

The door opened. Brady came inside first, and his gaze went directly to Riley. "This is not my fault. I'm sober. However, not everyone is, and, well . . ."

"Honey, I'm home!" Gunner announced as he pushed past Brady into the house. His eyes went to the food on the coffee table. "I told you they'd have the goods! Tallulah, I love your mother, and it's fucking good to see you."

Willa rolled her eyes. "Figures you'd be one of the drunk ones."

He grinned at her and winked. "Hey, baby," he said. "I missed you more."

West came in next, followed by Asa. They both appeared sober. West looked more concerned than anything. He whispered something to Brady, then headed over to Maggie.

"You can have my seat," I told Asa, since I was sitting by Ezmita.

He glanced at Ezmita and gave her an apologetic smile, then back to me. "I might not need to sit down just yet."

Just behind him, I heard Ryker curse, then laughter. Nash's laughter. My heart slammed inside my chest, and my throat felt as if someone had a vise grip on it. Unable to look away from the door, I watched as Ryker came inside with Nash, who was completely hammered and leaning on Ryker for support. My eyes couldn't take him in quickly enough. I inhaled sharply and felt light-headed. He straightened and pushed away from Ryker, then laughed again.

"The damn steps were moving. I'm good now," he slurred slightly, then, as if he realized where he was, his gaze moved across the room until he found me.

I couldn't move, much less speak. I just sat there staring back at him. I wanted to say so many things. I had gone over in my head hundreds of times all that I would say when I saw him again, but I wouldn't be saying them tonight.

"You're right," he said. "She is here." But I wasn't sure who he was talking to. He kept his eyes locked on me. Then he swayed, and Ryker reached out and grabbed him.

"You're drunk," Ryker told him. "You saw her, just like I promised. Now I'm taking you home to sleep this shit off."

He shoved Ryker then. "I'm fine. She can go. I'm not going anywhere," he slurred. "These are my friends. My fucking friends."

I stood up. Although it was clear he was drunk, his words were still like a slap in my face. You were honest when you were drunk. That's what I'd always heard. Maggie reached up and grabbed my arm. "Don't go. He's just had too much to drink."

"Don't matter how much I've had to drink. She can go," Nash shouted.

Ryker shoved him down into an empty chair and glared at him. "Shut the fuck up," he ordered.

I pulled my arm from Maggie's hold and walked around the group. "It's best that I leave. Thank you for inviting me, Riley. It was great to see everyone," I said with a smile I knew wasn't fooling anyone, but it was the best I could do.

"I'm sorry about this," Riley said.

I nodded. I knew she hadn't expected them to show up here.

"Let's go to lunch tomorrow," Willa called out to me as I reached the door.

"Okay," I replied, hoping I could make it out of here with my smile in place.

Several others called out how good it was to see me, and I managed to nod and reply. As I opened the door, Ryker muttered a curse, and I heard a noise behind me. I turned around to see the chair Nash had been sitting in fallen over on the floor and Nash coming directly at me.

Ryker grabbed for him, and Nash swung him off as his gaze stayed glued to me. I couldn't move. He didn't stop until he was so close to me his chest was touching mine, and I took a shaky breath. He reeked of whiskey.

Then he lowered his head and his lips brushed my ear. I trembled. My body reacted to him as if it belonged to him.

"You smell like vanilla. So fucking sweet," he whispered as his hand gripped my waist. "Just like I remember."

I didn't move, but a whimper escaped me.

He ran the tip of his nose across my cheek and back to my ear. "I want to take you to bed with me."

"Okay, that's enough. You're scaring her," Ryker said, and suddenly Nash was taken away from me. His eyes went to mine, and for a moment he looked panicked. He hadn't been scaring me, but he had been breaking me all over again.

"You good?" Brady asked me, and I managed a nod.

"I'll walk you to your car," West offered, walking around Ryker and Nash.

Nash moved then and grabbed West. "Don't fucking go near her!"

Startled by his angry outburst, I moved back quickly and grabbed the doorknob again. "That's okay," I said. "I . . .

I . . . need to go. Thanks again." I didn't wait for anyone to respond as I hurried out of the door and to my car. Thankful I had parked on the side of the road and not pulled into the driveway so that I could leave without needing someone inside to move their car. This night had been too much. My emotions felt raw and exposed. The pain in my chest was as intense as it had been the day Nash walked away from me.

Coming back was a mistake, but where did I belong? "Tallulah!" Nash's voice called out my name just as I reached my car. I froze, unsure if I should jump in my car and escape this or wait. Hearing much more from Nash was going to break me. Being here again was hard enough.

"I'm sorry. I'm drunk," his voice was closer now. Too close.

I turned slowly and looked at him. I had loved him for most of my life. He'd been my crush from the time I was a kid. Then he had become my first at so many things. Nash Lee had been my world until the day he wasn't. "Let's not do this," I begged softly. My heart couldn't take it.

"I can't let you walk away. I just . . . I just want to look at you. I spend my days wanting to look at you, to hear you talk, to see you smile." He groaned and ran a hand through his hair. "Even after you destroyed me, all I wanted was you. Why can't I get over you? Why can't I forget? Why, Tallulah?" his voice cracked and he swayed as he stared at me. His eyes so full of regret and pain. Emotions I understood too well.

"This isn't the time to talk about this," I told him gently. He wouldn't remember much in the morning. Although I wanted his words to be real. Not drunken ramblings.

"When you leave again it's going to rip me to fucking shreds. Because even though I don't have you, I know you're near. Just having you in the same town has helped me wake up every morning . . . God, I miss you."

"Nash!" West called out from the porch and then made his way down the stairs and toward us. He would take Nash inside and I would drive away. My heart couldn't take much more of the things Nash was saying and I knew it was for the best that West stopped this but a big part of me wanted to throw myself into Nash's arms and cry.

"That's enough," West said, coming up behind him. "You want to talk to her, then do it sober. Not like this. This isn't fucking fair and you'll regret it."

Nash's stricken expression as he looked at me made it hard to breathe my chest hurt so badly. He nodded his head then in agreement. "Yeah, I've had too much to drink," he agreed.

"Let's go," West took his arm then and Nash turned around slowly, looking back at me as he did.

"I might be drunk but what I said, that's all true," he said before stumbling back toward the house with West.

He had hurt me worse than I'd ever been hurt. Nash had claimed I destroyed him but he had been the one to do the damage. Yet, looking at him tonight when he wasn't holding up a wall to protect himself, something in me cracked. I began to understand him more. If only he could say those things sober.

CHAPTER FIVE

NASH

The sound of a door closing stirred me, and then the pounding of my head caused me to wince. What the fuck had I done?

"Why is Nash here, Mommy?" a voice asked.

I opened my eyes to see where the hell I was when the sunlight caused me to curse and slam them back shut again.

"He slept here last night on the sofa and is waking up grumpy," Riley replied.

I was at Brady and Riley's house.

We had gone to the bar. I'd drunk a lot.

Then we'd come here . . . Oh, hell.

Groaning, I covered my face.

"And now he is remembering why drinking whiskey is a bad idea," Riley said.

"Is he sick?" Bryony asked.

"Yup," Riley replied.

"Where's Daddy? Did he drink whiskey too?"

"No, he's in the shower. I'll get Nash some coffee. Go take your overnight bag to your room and put your things away."

"Are we going to the pool today?" Bryony asked.

"Yes."

Finally the talking stopped, and I gave it a few minutes before opening my eyes again. Slowly this time and sitting up. My mouth felt like sandpaper. How much fucking whiskey had I drunk? And what the hell . . . Oh, fuck.

"Riley." I called out her name, although it sounded like a grunt.

"Yes?" she replied, stepping back into the living room.

"Was she here?" I asked.

"Oh yes, and you were in rare form. I can honestly say I've never seen you that kind of drunk."

"Damn," I muttered, dropping my head into my hands.

"He's awake." Brady's voice entered the room.

"Unfortunately," I groaned.

Brady let out a heavy sigh. "We should have cut you off sooner. Didn't realize you'd had so many until it was too late."

"What time is it?" I asked.

"After nine, but Asa went to the field house for early morning workouts," Brady replied.

"Great," I muttered.

Riley walked back into the room with a cup of coffee and a pill in her hand. "Take this and drink the coffee. Then go home and shower because you stink. Once you're recovered, you need to go find Tallulah. I am over this ridiculous standoff you two are doing. I know what happened, and it's not what you think. Get over there and talk to her for *all* of our sakes."

I took the aspirin and popped it in my mouth, then washed it down with the coffee. Glancing up at Riley, I saw she had her hands on her hips and was glaring down at me. "She's not gonna want to see me after last night."

Riley rolled her eyes. "Oh, please. You were drunk. She knows that. She will want to see sober Nash. Now get yourself together."

Brady sat down in the chair across from me, and Riley walked out of the room. I finished my coffee in silence. I wasn't sure what all I'd said last night, but I did remember getting up in her face and smelling her like a damn crazed man. She'd smelled like Tallulah. God, I'd missed her.

"How bad was I?" I asked Brady.

He shrugged. "Other than the fact you tried to eat her

up, not bad at all. She let you get close and didn't move, so that says something. I'm not sure what the hell you were whispering in her ear, but she wasn't pushing you away."

"She ran out of here," I reminded him.

He laughed. "Yeah, she did. You yelled at West like a jealous crazed idiot and scared the shit out of her."

"Fuck," I muttered again, then set my cup down and stood up. "I need to go. Where's my keys?"

Brady nodded toward the door. "On the key rack," he said.

I folded up the cover that had been thrown over me and then walked to get my keys. "Thanks for letting me crash," I told him.

Brady smirked. "I don't think I had an option. You passed out."

Shaking my head, I left Brady's. I had to get something in my stomach, and Riley was right: I stunk.

Asa wasn't home when I pulled into the drive, and I was glad. Talking hurt my head. Listening hurt my head. Hell, breathing hurt my head. The hot shower, however, did give me some relief—or the pain medicine Riley had given me had started to work.

Once I no longer smelled of whiskey and smoke, I made myself some cheese toast. Food helped improve my hangover as well. Riley was right, I needed to go talk to Tallulah. Problem was I didn't know where to fucking start. It had been thirteen months, twenty-one days, and seven hours since I had walked out of her office in Chicago. Seeing her last night didn't count because my memories were blurry at best.

If after all that time she still consumed my thoughts, didn't that mean something? I had to give her a chance to tell me why I'd walked in on her kissing that stupid fucker. I needed to know if she'd been with him this year. Had they dated? Had she been seeing someone? Could I handle it if she had been?

"Damn," I growled, standing up and slamming my palm down on the table. Just thinking about it twisted me up inside so tightly I couldn't take a deep breath.

My doorbell rang, interrupting my breakdown, and my head snapped up to glare at the door as if it had offended me. I wasn't in the mood for another pep talk from one of my friends. Couldn't they leave me alone for five minutes to think? I had too much to deal with right now, and they weren't making it any better.

Stalking to the door, I jerked it open, ready to send away whoever had decided to stop by and butt into my life, when my eyes locked on Tallulah's. All my anger vanished, and I stood there staring at her. She had come to me.

I wasn't sure that was a good thing. It was me who should have gone to apologize to her. What if she was here to tell me good-bye?

"Feeling okay?" she asked with a sympathetic half smile.

I shrugged and ran my hand through my hair before stepping back. "Better than I deserve," I admitted. "Come in."

She looked hesitant at first, but she walked inside and the scent of vanilla wafted past me. I had to fist my hands to keep from reaching out and grabbing her.

"You got a new sofa and a new truck," she said, looking at the gray leather sofa.

"New bed, too," I replied.

She forced a smile and glanced back at me. "That's unlike you," she said. "Buying new stuff like that."

"I almost had the shower torn out and replaced," I admitted.

Her eyebrows shot up. "Why? This house isn't that old."

With a sigh, I looked at the gray sofa. "Wasn't about needing new ones. I just couldn't deal with anything that we had . . . that reminded me of . . . being with you."

"Oh," she whispered.

"The memories, they had wrecked me. Every damn day. I thought getting new ones would help."

"Did it?" she asked softly.

I looked back at her. "No."

She tucked a strand of hair behind her ear and took a deep breath. "Look, Nash, I didn't come back to town to cause problems. I came because that was your handwriting on that envelope. I thought maybe you were ready to talk, but after last night . . ." She paused and pressed her lips together as if unsure what to say next.

"I was a drunk asshole last night. I did want you to come," I told her.

Her lips pooched as she let out a breath. "Okay," she said. "Does that mean you want to hear what happened?"

I didn't know if I could. Or if it even mattered anymore. She was here in my house. The house I had bought for us. She was back where she belonged, and I realized I didn't give a damn about what happened. I just didn't want her to leave me.

"Depends," I replied, then I took a step toward her. "Do you still love me?"

She let out a short, breathy laugh. "You have no idea how I wish I didn't. How I tried so hard not to love you. But I'm afraid I always will . . . love you."

I closed the space between us and ran a hand up her arm. "Then that's all I care about. If I can have you, I don't care about the fucking past. I just want you back. I'm not complete without you, Tallulah."

Her eyes filled with unshed tears, and she let out a small sob. "Really?"

"Yeah, really. I'll sell this house. Put it on the market tomorrow and move to Chicago."

Her eyes widened, and a tear ran down her face. "You love your job," she said.

I cupped her face with both hands. "No, I love you. Just you. Nothing else matters if you're not there."

I wiped away the tears now flowing freely down her face with my thumbs, then pressed my lips to hers. God, how I had missed this. My chest felt like it may burst. Her sweet taste intoxicated me, and I wrapped my arms around her to hold her against me. I'd never let her go again. She was my life.

Tallulah broke the kiss, and I looked down into her eyes.

"I want to come home," she said. "Chicago isn't my home. You are."

I shook my head. "No, I'm not letting you give that job up for me."

She laughed. "I was already planning on leaving the job and coming back before today. I miss Lawton. I miss our life here."

"Are you positive that's what you want? Because I swear to God I will happily follow you to fucking Antarctica if that's where you want to go."

Her laughter filled me, and the darkness that had become a part of me was gone. "That won't be necessary," she said, then pressed another kiss to my lips. "This house, our house, right here in Lawton, is exactly where I want to be."

I left a trail of kisses from her mouth to her ear, then whispered, "If that's the case, then I have a new bed I want to show you."

Tallulah's laughter was the sweetest damn thing in the world.

WEST AND MAGGIE

CHAPTER ONE

WEST

I stood in the parking lot that now covered the grassy wooded area where we had once parked our trucks. The only tree still standing was the one I had asked Nash and Ryker not to take down. I'd even promised a yearly donation to the new football complex just to keep that tree. My plan for tonight had been to bring Maggie here, to that tree where I had first kissed her, and ask her to marry me.

My chest tightened thinking of how everything had changed. The ache of loss that had slowly eased over the years since my father's death was now throbbing painfully. So many times since losing Dad, my mother's actions had hurt me far deeper than I'd thought imaginable. She'd made decisions that would have destroyed me had Maggie not been there beside me.

Once I had thought Maggie must have been an angel God had sent to me when I was facing the darkest days of my life. Now I *knew* she was. She was the reason I woke up every morning. Since the first time she opened her mouth and spoke to me, I had been hers. I hadn't known it back then, but I had been. She'd owned me before I even realized it.

Tonight had been something I'd been planning for months. The diamond I'd worked and saved to buy had been burning a hole in my pocket. Every time she smiled at me, I had fought the urge to drop to my knee and ask her to marry me. I had been going to get that moment tonight. I had made sure it would be perfect. That she would remember it and tell our grandchildren about it one day.

My eyes dropped to the phone in my hand, and I knew that wasn't going to happen now. The phone call I had received three hours ago from my mother had changed everything. Somehow she had managed to hit me with yet another blow, reminding me she was no longer the mother from my youth. She wasn't the woman my dad had adored.

Her last name was no longer Ashby. I flinched as the pain sliced through me. The memories of a childhood that felt as if it were another lifetime now all flooded me. The way my mother had loved my father so fiercely and the way he had cherished her. My parents' love had been the reason I believed in it.

Facing the fact that the mother I knew had also died that day when my father took his last breath wasn't easy, but with Maggie in my arms I had been able to accept it. Or at least I had thought I had accepted it. It had been over a year since I had seen my mother, but only because she canceled plans, not me. Thanksgiving she'd been on a cruise with friends. Christmas she had gone skiing in Colorado.

Now I knew the truth. It hadn't been friends she had been with. It hadn't been plural at all. She'd been with a man. A man I had never met. A man she had married last week in Hawaii. I knew nothing more because I had simply ended the call while she was still talking. I couldn't listen to her happy voice talking about this man she kept praising and how much I would like him. How could she do this? Who was she? How did someone change so completely? She had loved my dad. That was not something anyone could fake. I'd witnessed it and lived in the security of my parents' love until the day he left this earth.

My phone rang, and Maggie's name lit up the screen. She was who I went to when I needed strength. Holding her in my arms always fixed all my problems. Nothing mattered if I had her with me. But this . . .

Not this.

And not now.

I couldn't tell her how I'd been going to ask her to marry me. I couldn't tell her about my mother. Because the truth was I no longer believed love was forever. People changed, and I had watched it with my mother now for years. Marriage no longer felt like something full of promise and a future.

It fucking terrified me.

Losing my mom to this person she had become was one thing.

But if Maggie changed. If I lost Maggie like that, how would I keep on living? Maggie was my heart. How did one go on when they lost their heart?

I pressed ignore on the phone and slipped it into my pocket.

Right now I needed space. Even from her.

CHAPTER TWO

MAGGIE

I dropped my phone back onto the table and finished nibbling the saltine cracker in my hand, hoping to ease the turmoil in my stomach. Aunt Coralee was gone to the grocery store, and I was thankful she went early so that I had time alone to deal with my nausea. This was only the third day that I'd been sick. I had hoped before I started feeling bad that I'd get the chance to tell West.

The positive pregnancy test I'd gotten two weeks ago had been a shock. I'd been taking birth control for years, and I had never had one late period. So when my period was a full seven days late, I had taken a test, not truly expecting it to be positive.

Then I had taken three more, different kinds, only to get the exact same answer. We were going to have a baby. This wasn't planned, but the more it had sunk in, the more excited I had become. We had graduated with our bachelor's degrees, both found jobs, and were moving from Atlanta to Savannah next month to begin our new life there.

We often spoke about our future, and I wasn't insecure about West's feelings for me. However, every time the diamond ring on Riley's hand flashed in the light, I felt a pang of envy. I hated that too. I shouldn't feel anything but happiness for her and Brady. I loved them both. I wanted that for them.

I studied my bare ring finger and felt tears sting my eyes. I was being silly, and I knew it. West didn't have to put a ring on my finger. Not now, at least. Maybe one day. When he was ready.

I dropped a hand to my stomach and thought of the life inside me. As much as I wanted this baby, I did not want it to be the reason he asked me to marry him. I wanted that to be something he did because he was ready for me to have his last name. We talked about our future all the time, and I knew he planned on ours being together. Deep down, I had always thought once we graduated college he'd propose.

When he didn't, I was fine with it and didn't think about it too much. Until now. Riley and Brady were planning a wedding, and I was sneaking around eating saltine crackers and sipping Sprite. My hormones were doing crazy things right now. That had to be why I was on the verge of tears and insecure all of a sudden.

I stood up from the table and cleared away the evidence of my meager meal, then stood there a moment as another wave of nausea went through me. It was worse today than it had been yesterday. I wasn't sure I could hide this much longer. Not if it got worse every day. I hadn't thrown up yet, but this morning had been the first time I thought I was going to. I'd turned on the water in the bathroom and stared at myself for several minutes, waiting for it to happen, hoping the running water would cover up the sound of my heaving.

It never came, and I eventually went back to my room and lay down. The doorbell rang, and I took a deep breath, hoping the crackers were going to stay down, before I walked to the living room to answer the door. I was home alone for now, with Aunt Coralee grocery shopping and West being gone. I had no idea where he was because he wasn't answering his cell phone. I'd worry about that if I didn't hear from him in another hour or so.

I opened the door, not checking to see who it was. Lawton was small and safe. Checking to see who was on the other side of the door was never something anyone thought to do here. It was something I missed about living here. I may not have grown up here, but Lawton was my home. This house was the first home I had felt safe in. My father had made it impossible to feel safe.

A started to say hello, but no words came when the guy whose back had been all I could see since he was looking out toward the street turned to face me. It took me a moment. The face was familiar, yet I wasn't sure why. I studied him a moment, unsure if I should know him. Was he someone that Brady knew?

"Maggie." He said my name, and a smile tugged at the corner of his lips. The way his eyes twinkled when he did so was something I did recognize. My mouth fell open in surprise as I stared back at the boy from my childhood. The kid next door that I couldn't remember ever meeting because I had just always known him. He was in every memory I had as a kid and in most all of them until the day I left that house and never returned.

"Tate?" I said in a whisper, almost unsure that this was who I thought it was.

He chuckled then, and I knew that sound. It was deeper now and belonged to a grown man not the boy I remembered. It was him. But why? How?

I shook my head and laughed. "What?" I asked, unsure how to finish that question. I hadn't thought of Tate in years. Most of my memories from the house I had grown up in I had blocked out. Kept in a dark corner that I didn't explore. Unfortunately, Tate had been shoved away with them. Even though he had been my first best friend and back then possibly my only real friend.

He gave me a crooked grin. "What am I doing here?" he asked for me.

I managed a nod.

He sighed then and ran a hand through his blond hair. It hadn't darkened over the years and was still as pale as it had been when we were younger. "That's a good question, Mags," he said, then lifted his shoulders. "I've been asking myself the same damn thing the entire drive here."

That did nothing to answer my question. I waited, and he glanced back at the car in the driveway. It was a shiny black Mercedes. Tate's family was wealthy, and I wouldn't expect him to drive anything less impressive. Even if he was . . . twenty-four now? Or was he twenty-three? I couldn't remember.

"You're talking again. That's good," he said.

I didn't reply because I wasn't sure what to say. This was so strange.

"Can we go get some coffee? Or maybe lunch? To talk," he asked, looking at me hopefully.

"Did you come to Lawton to see me?" I asked him finally.

He flashed me that grin again. "Yeah, Mags. I did. I can explain myself if you'll come with me to get some food." His gaze dropped to my hands then, and I saw something that seemed awfully close to relief in his eyes.

"I, uh . . ." I paused and tried to remember where I had left my phone. "I need to call," I started, then stopped again. Referring to West as my boyfriend seemed strange. We were more than that. Especially now. We may not be engaged, but we were going to be parents. That was more than a simple boyfriend. "Let me get my phone. Uh, come on in a second," I told him, then walked back to the kitchen to find my cell phone still on the table.

Picking it up I saw no missed calls. There was one text from Aunt Coralee asking me how I felt about chicken Parmesan for dinner. I quickly responded that it sounded great to me.

Then I typed out a text to West telling him to call me. Explaining Tate and his sudden appearance felt strange in a text. Especially when I didn't even know what to think of it.

I hit send, then went back to tell Tate that lunch would be fine.

CHAPTER THREE

WEST

"Thought I might find you here." Brady's voice didn't surprise me. I had heard a vehicle drive up and the door slam closed. I figured it was him when I ignored his last two texts.

"Yeah," I replied.

He came to stand beside me, but I couldn't count on him remaining silent. He always talked too damn much.

"Can't imagine you're getting cold feet on this. But then I was supposed to get the final plan from you this morning for tonight, and I've not heard from you. Not sure what to think now."

Brady was the only person I'd told about my plans to propose to Maggie tonight. I had needed him to set some things up for me, and I'd asked him weeks ago. I had assumed he'd have questions. Even if I wasn't in the mood to talk about this.

"Don't want to talk right now," I told him.

He sighed, but I knew that wasn't going to shut him up. "Don't care," he replied. "You may be my best friend, but Maggie is my cousin. If you're planning on hurting her, I need to know now, so I can sufficiently beat your ass and some sense into you."

I shot him an annoyed glare. "I'd never hurt her."

He raised his eyebrows at me as if he wasn't so sure. "You've been together seven years. You're living together. Planning your future together. Why the fuck have you waited so long to put a ring on her finger?"

Brady could piss me off enough to get me to talk. He was good at that. "Because we both needed to get our degrees and there wasn't time to focus on planning a wedding. Maggie never brought it up or even hinted she wanted to be engaged. I was following her lead."

Brady let out a hard, short laugh that held little amusement. "I'd say moving in together is a fucking hint."

I knew that just as I knew she was ready to take the next step. But I wanted that to be special. I wanted the memory of my asking her to marry me to be something she always remembered fondly. How was I supposed to do that when my head was messed the fuck up? My mom was married. It was like my dad had never existed. She barely knew me anymore.

"Right now isn't the time," I said.

"When will be the right time?" he shot back at me.

I shrugged. I didn't know. I had too many other things to deal with right now. Maggie wasn't pressing me for a ring.

"Maggie isn't expecting this. She's not asking for it."

Brady sighed heavily. "When has Maggie ever pressed anyone for anything? I sure as hell can't think of a time. She takes what is given to her and never expects more. Problem is I expect more for her. She's the closest thing I have to a sibling, and I want to see her have it all."

I jerked my gaze from the field and leveled it on Brady. No one wanted more for Maggie than I did. "She is my fucking world," I shouted at him, angry at his assumption I didn't want her to have everything.

He shrugged. "Then act like it," he replied, then turned and walked away, leaving me standing there alone again. I waited until he climbed into his truck and drove away before heading to my own to leave. Maggie had texted and called. I needed to respond. She'd get worried.

Before I drove off, I texted her:

On my way back to the house.

Then I started the truck and pulled out of the parking lot.

I'm not at the house. I tried to call you. I am at lunch with an old friend. A very old friend. It's a long story. I'll explain later.

Glancing down, I read her response. What the hell? She didn't have very old friends. Not in Lawton. I pulled over to the side of the road and checked Life360 to find her location. I didn't want an explanation later. I wanted to see Maggie. Now. I needed to see her. It was the only thing that would make the ache inside me ease. It always had been.

CHAPTER FOUR

MAGGIE

Tate sat across from me at Wicks. The outdoor seating here was the best in town, and I wanted to be in clear view. I wasn't doing anything wrong, but being here with a guy and not being able to explain it to West felt off. Taking a sip of my water, I waited until Tate had ordered his lunch.

When the waitress walked away, he looked back at me and grinned.

"I looked for you, you know. For years after you left. I tried to find out where you had gone. Then I let it go." He paused and shook his head. "But a week ago I realized maybe I hadn't. Let you go. I'm . . . I'm engaged." He stopped then and looked at me.

"Congratulations," I said, feeling some relief. I hadn't been sure what he was here to say to me or why he felt like he needed to see me other than to catch up.

He did a small sigh mixed with a laugh, as if that wasn't what he wanted to hear. "I thought coming to see you would give me the closure that I needed. You were my best friend, then you were the girl who was out of my league, and I had to watch you date other boys. Junior high sucked." He laughed. "But we still met out by the pond and talked as if life hadn't changed. I had that. I still had a part of you. You were my first love, and although that love was unrequited, it was powerful for me. One day you were there and then you were gone. Even before leaving school and moving, you pulled away from me. From life. I never got to say good-bye, and next weekend I'm supposed to get married. But for the past month all I can think about is what if she's not the one? What if she is a stand-in? What if I don't love her as much as I loved . . . you?"

I sat there, my hands fisted in the napkin in my lap, wishing for a way to escape this. What was I supposed to say to him? Yes, a part of me had known back then that Tate had feelings for me. He had always just been my friend, and I hadn't wanted that to change. But time went on, and it did. When I had moved to Lawton I hadn't thought of him once. He hadn't been more than a part of my past. A past I didn't dwell on.

"Tate," I said, trying to think of the right thing to say and not sure what that might be. "I, uh, I think you're just nervous. You asked her to marry you. That means something. Something much bigger than a childhood crush. We never had more than a friendship. Could it be that you're just worried about getting married and you're projecting that onto me? Because I didn't say good-bye?"

He shook his head. "No," he replied firmly. "I still dream about you, Mags. That's not some childhood crush."

I opened my mouth to argue, but my words were cut off.

"That sounds like your problem. Not hers." West's deep voice came from behind me just as his hand landed on my shoulder.

Tate looked from me to the man standing behind me. "Excuse me?" Tate asked, a touch of irritation in his expression.

"You heard me," West replied. "Let's go, Maggie." The possessiveness in his tone left no room for argument, and honestly, I was glad he was here. I hadn't expected this, and I was unsure how to handle it.

"We've not been introduced," Tate said, standing up

and holding out his hand. "I'm an old friend of Maggie's. Tate Morris."

West didn't reach out to shake Tate's hand. Instead his hand squeezed my shoulder. "An old friend who's dreaming about her." West's tone held a warning there I hoped Tate picked up on.

"We have a past," Tate replied in a challenging tone.

I stood up then. If I didn't end this, then it was going to get nasty. I could feel the tension coming off West, and he wasn't himself. Something was wrong. There was an anger just below the surface I didn't think had to do with Tate. West trusted me. It was something more.

West's hand moved to my back, and he kissed my temple. "Let's go," he told me.

"We were having lunch. She's not eaten yet," Tate argued.

West's entire body went rigid. He was controlling his temper, but I could feel it being pushed too far. "Maggie is mine," he said in a low, hard tone. His jaw was clenched, and I put my hand on his chest to calm him.

"Tate, it was good to see you again. Congratulations on your upcoming wedding," I told him. "But we should be going," I added, then pushed for West to move and break his glare, which was leveled at Tate.

I didn't wait for Tate to say more, and thankfully West moved then, keeping his hand on my back as we made our way back inside Wicks toward the exit.

"Show me your server," he said.

I looked over at the girl who had taken our order and pointed at her. He dropped his hand from my back and walked over to her. I watched as he handed her money, then he headed back to me.

"No man is buying you anything but me," he said simply, then put his hand on my back again and led me out to the parking lot.

I wanted to explain all of this to him. I just wasn't sure where to start. When we reached his truck, he didn't open the passenger door like I expected but pressed my back against it instead. His hands flattened against the truck on each side of my head as his eyes locked on mine.

"No man gets to talk to you like that," he said just before his mouth lowered to cover mine. His kiss was more forceful than usual, but I knew it was because of the scene we'd just had. I slid my hands up his chest and fisted his shirt, holding him to me, reassuring him that no man would ever have me but him. He should know that by now.

When he broke the kiss, he rested his forehead on mine and closed his eyes.

"Something else is wrong, West," I said softly. "I know you. What is it?"

He sighed heavily, then dropped his hands and stepped back from me. "Let's go. I want to be alone with you."

I didn't push, but I would later.

CHAPTER FIVE

WEST

I lay in bed listening to Maggie's breathing and watching her sleep. She'd fallen asleep after we had quietly made love for over an hour in her blue bedroom at the Higgenses' house. Tonight I should be holding my fiancée. There should be a ring on her finger.

But instead it was like any other night.

I reached for her left hand and gently held it in my much larger palm. Her bare ring finger caused an empty feeling to expand inside me. I'd let my mother's actions ruin tonight. Brady had barely spoken to me at dinner. When our eyes did meet, I could see the disapproval in them. He didn't understand, and he had the wrong damn idea in his head. There was nothing in this world I wanted more than Maggie. Making her my wife, giving her my last name, that was all in my plans.

My dad had known she was the one for me before I'd been willing to admit it. He'd love knowing she was going to be an Ashby. He had told me she was the kind of girl you held on to and I needed to make her mine. I hoped Maggie was right and he could see us now. That heaven she believed in I wasn't positive about, but I liked thinking Dad was watching us and smiling.

Laying Maggie's hand back down, I eased out of bed. She was a heavy sleeper, but I still moved quietly. My inner demons shouldn't keep her awake too. Walking over to the window, I stared outside at the darkness lit by the streetlights.

Tomorrow Maggie would make me talk. She'd watched me all day with that all-too-knowing look. I couldn't hide anything from her. I figured she hadn't pushed me simply because of the jackass guy who had shown up to try and take what was mine. My anger at the idea of another man saying things like that to Maggie ignited again, and I had to take a deep breath to shove that down.

He was gone now, and I had other shit to deal with: getting my head clear and my fucking fears under control so I could move forward with Maggie. Brady was right. It was past time. If my mother hadn't gone from a devoted, loving, adoring wife and mother to this person I no longer know, I would be engaged to Maggie.

"You distracted me with sex. Now it's time talk to me." Maggie's soft voice broke the silence, and I turned to see her watching me. She was so damn beautiful. The thought of her changing, of her love for me fading, of what we have ending twisted my insides so tightly it made me ill.

"Please, West," she said, sitting up in bed, her eyes never leaving mine.

I'd lost both parents the day my father died. I hadn't known it then, but soon enough it had become obvious. Maggie had been my only constant. She was more than the woman I loved; she was my life. If I lost her. If she were to die, would I change? My chest ached inside me at the idea of a world without Maggie in it.

Yes, I would change. I'd lose my soul. She'd take it with her. Was that what had happened to my mother? Had her love for my dad been so intense that she couldn't be the same person when he was gone, even for me?

As a kid, that had been the most painful truth. But as Maggie stood up and walked over to me, wrapping a sheet around her naked body, I understood. It wasn't right, but I did understand it. Losing Maggie would destroy me. I needed there to be a God. I needed to start praying that he take me first.

"West," she whispered as she reached me, touching my arm.

I pulled her against me and held her there. Feeling the beat of her heart, the rise and fall of her chest as she breathed. Calming myself with knowing she was mine. She was alive.

"My mother got married again," I told her.

The sharp intake of breath from Maggie told me that she understood my pain. Her arms tightened around me and held me.

"She hasn't seen me in a year, but she's married." I said the words, realizing that was possibly what hurt the worst.

Maggie tilted her head back to look up at me. "I'm sorry," she said simply. It was her way. She never said words to sugarcoat things. I loved that about her.

"It fucking hurts," I said, looking down into her eyes. "But I realized something tonight. Something I've battled with and didn't understand until now."

Maggie waited for me to say more.

"I was her son, but she loved my father so fiercely that he was her world. He was her home. Losing him destroyed her, and . . . I can see how it did." I reached up and cupped her face in my hand. "If she loved him the way I love you, then it makes it easier to accept. I couldn't survive losing you, Maggie."

She turned her head to kiss my palm, then looked back up at me. "You'll never lose me," she replied.

I couldn't bring myself to even voice the fear of her dying before me. I just nodded my head once and then covered her mouth with mine. What I felt for her was bigger than even I could describe. It was more than simply love. There were no words for it, but I'd spend my lifetime showing her what I couldn't express.

CHAPTER SIX

MAGGIE

I didn't have much time to worry about the running water being loud enough to drown out the sound of my vomiting. All I could do at the moment was grip the toilet and pray this ended soon. West had still been in bed sleeping when my eyes opened this morning and the first wave of nausea hit me. I had been as quiet as I could, but getting to the bathroom quickly had been my first priority.

Last night after I had led West back to the bed, I had lain awake until his breathing had told me he'd fallen asleep. He was hurting, and when he hurt, so did I. Maybe he understood his mother's actions now, but I wasn't sure that I ever would. Telling him that didn't help matters, though. I had remained silent and let him talk. That was what he needed most.

The thought of West dying was something I didn't want to consider. As much as I loved my aunt Coralee, Brady, and even my uncle Boone, West was my family. He was where my home was. Wherever he was, I wanted to be. This child inside of me was a part of him. I already loved it just as fiercely, and no loss or pain would change that.

I sat back on my heels and took a deep breath to make sure I was done before standing up and going over to the sink to wash my mouth out. I stared at my reflection. My face was far too pale, and West was going to notice. Hopefully a hot shower would put some color in my cheeks. I went to the tub and turned on the water. Closing my eyes tightly, I focused on breathing as more nausea waves hit me. This was worse than a stomach virus. Throwing up didn't even ease it.

I glanced back down at the toilet, wondering if I should stay close to it for a few more minutes, but decided there was nothing else inside of me. I had cleared that out already. Instead I took off my clothing and stepped into the warmth of the running water. It was nice. The sickness didn't go away, but it was soothed some. Maybe I should stay in here all morning.

Taking my time, I finished washing my hair and then

my body. When I was done, I was tempted to stand under the water until it ran cold. But that would be unfair to West and Aunt Coralee if they needed to shower.

With one last blast of the warmth, I turned it off and stepped out to dry off. My nausea was still there, but I did feel clean. Opening the bathroom door, I stepped out to see West standing there staring at me. His arms were crossed over his chest and his jaw clenched tight. It was his angry stance.

It was a rare moment that it was ever directed at me. The last time I got that look from him was because I'd walked back to my apartment alone from class in the dark and not called him to tell him I needed a ride. He'd been furious with me then and we'd fought about it for maybe thirty minutes. Then we'd ended up not making it to the bedroom and made up on the sofa.

This morning I didn't feel well enough to figure out what had caused this reaction.

"What?" I asked, feeling weak.

He said nothing, but his gaze studied my face and I saw the muscles in his neck flex. I started to demand a reason for this when his eyes dropped to my stomach. The nausea intensified as realization sank in. He had heard me. He knew.

Wrapped in a towel, I walked past him toward the

bedroom. I went directly to the closet, where the suitcase lay open. I wasn't going to talk first. I had imagined many reactions from West when I told him, but this was not one of them.

The bedroom door clicked shut as I picked up a pair of panties.

"I heard you, Maggie." He stated what I had already figured out.

Turning around, I looked at him. "Okay," I replied.

"I'm assuming it's not a stomach virus."

"Nope," I said.

"Have you taken a test?"

"Several."

He let out a deep sigh and ran his hand through his hair. "Were you planning on telling me?"

"Of course. I just wanted it to be after this was over."

He muttered a curse and walked over to stare out the window. Tears filled my eyes without warning, and I fisted the panties in my hand, trying hard to fight off my need to break down. I would cry about this, but I didn't want to do it in front of him. The feeling of loneliness weighed down on me, and I turned back toward my closet before the first tears fell.

A sob escaped me, and I let the panties fall back into the suitcase so I could cover my face. There was no stopping the emotions bursting free now.

"Maggie." West's voice was softer. The anger that had been in his expression wasn't echoed in his tone, but I didn't look back at him.

His arms came around me and pulled me to his chest. That only made the sobbing worse. "Please don't cry. I didn't mean to make you cry. I was just taken by surprise. I wasn't expecting this. I handled it wrong."

I was trying to stop crying, but it was a battle I wasn't winning. No matter how hard I tried, more sobs broke free. It was making my nausea worse. We hadn't talked about kids. We'd talked about where we wanted to live and the places we wanted to visit. We'd shared our dreams, but we'd never talked about kids.

It wasn't until now that I wondered why.

CHAPTER SEVEN

WEST

Maggie's sobs were breaking my heart. Knowing I'd made her cry like this had me so damn twisted up I couldn't take a deep breath. I had to calm her down. I'd never heard her this upset, and I never wanted to again.

Taking her arms, I turned her around and wrapped my arms back around her. "Please, baby. Stop crying. I'm sorry. Just please stop this. You're killing me," I pleaded.

She nodded her head against my chest and hiccupped, struggling to control her outburst. I kissed the top of her head. This wasn't like Maggie. Normally when we fought or got into an argument she held her own. She was fiery and tough. That was what I expected from her. Not this.

"I should," she said, then hiccupped, "have told you."

She thought I was mad because she hadn't told me. Hell, I wasn't sure I had been mad. More frustrated about the way it was all playing out. This wasn't how it was supposed to happen. We were supposed to get engaged and married. I wanted her all to myself for a few years. Maybe more. I didn't want to share her.

Yes, it was fucking selfish, but it was the truth.

More than that, I didn't want her to think when I proposed that it was because she was pregnant. That wasn't the memory I wanted her to have. She was supposed to get the perfect story to tell our grandkids. Not this.

I ran my hand down her damp head. "It's okay. Everything is going to be fine," I reassured her.

She nodded and sniffled. The sobbing had stopped, and I had never been more fucking thankful. That shit was soul-crushing. I couldn't handle it. If anyone else had made her cry like that, I'd have killed them.

"It's my fault. I forgot it was time for another shot. I didn't put it on my calendar," she said, then sniffled again before looking up at me.

I tucked the wet hair hanging over her face behind her ear. "It's okay," I repeated.

Her eyes were red and puffy as she frowned. "You were angry. It's not okay."

I ran my thumb over her lips. "I was surprised. I reacted like an ass, but I would have handled it better if I'd known it would upset you like this."

Her bottom lip trembled. "We never talked about kids, but I want this baby, and . . . and I'm happy about it. Scared but happy."

A baby. Just hearing her say it was terrifying. But I couldn't say that. She was scared, and I had to be the one to ease her fears.

"It's a part of you. I want it too." That was the truth. Anything that was a part of Maggie, I wanted.

"It's a part of you, too. It's both of us. We made it together." There was a slight tug at the corner of her lips.

"You should start praying now it's a girl and nothing like me," I told her.

She laughed then, and the sound was what I needed to mend the pain her crying had caused. Maggie happy was what I needed to keep my world centered.

She swallowed hard and took a deep breath, then swayed slightly. I pulled her tighter against me. "What's wrong?" I asked, feeling panicked and completely useless.

"Nausea and I'm weak. I need to eat something. It'll help," she said softly.

I picked her up and started for the door. "On it," I assured her.

"West, I can walk," she said with a small laugh.

"Maybe, but I need you to let me carry you. Please," I replied. The idea of her fainting or getting hurt was more than I could deal with at the moment. I'd just been informed I was going to be a dad. My reason for living had broken down on me and cried pitifully. I was currently damaged and needed to hold her.

"What if Aunt Coralee sees us?" she asked.

"Not real worried about her at the moment. Just you. Always you," I told her, then pressed a kiss to the tip of her nose.

CHAPTER EIGHT

MAGGIE

I didn't cry much. It was rare. West wasn't used to it, and the way he had gone from angry to hovering over me so quickly had been because of the tears. I knew that. He was beating himself up about making me cry. I felt silly for crying now. My emotions were heightened lately.

When Riley had called and asked me to go shopping with her and Bryony then get ice cream, West had surprised me by encouraging it. After he had carried me to breakfast and fixed me dry toast and orange juice then dried my hair for me, I hadn't expected him to let me out of his sight all day.

Bryony had been little when Brady and Riley began

dating. I had watched her grow up, and she called me Aunt Maggie. Brady had become a dad so easily, as if he were born for the role. Bryony saw him as just that. Her dad. They were something we were used to, as if it had always been.

Being with them today, though, made me see things differently. I paid more attention. I watched as Riley interacted with her daughter. When they laughed together, my heart squeezed. When they told me stories about things that I had missed while in college and finished each other's sentences, I felt my chest swell. I realized I was close to crying again. The simple fact that I was going to have this too, I was going to get to experience this, was just truly sinking in.

On our drive back to Lawton from our shopping day in Cullman, I felt my eyes grow heavy, and I couldn't keep from closing them. It wasn't until the car stopped that I realized I had fallen asleep. We weren't parked outside the house, though. We were in the parking lot of the field. I looked at Riley, confused.

"Wake up, sleepyhead," she teased.

"Are we meeting up with everyone here?" I asked her, my thoughts still groggy from a much deeper sleep than I'd realized.

"No, West just wanted me to drop you off with him. He's been up here working. I think y'all are going to go get dinner. I need to take Coralee some things, so I'll drop off your purchases there."

The smile on Riley's face was strange, as if she was trying to control it from being too bright. I glanced in the backseat to see that Bryony had also fallen asleep. "Sorry I fell asleep on you," I told Riley.

"No worries. I enjoyed the silence. I had fun today. I'll give you a call tomorrow," she told me.

Reaching down, I picked up my purse. "Thanks for the invite."

She was still beaming at me when I closed the car door, and I waved once more before she drove off. Turning around, I started toward the stadium lights and the facility to see if I could find West without calling him.

Just before I reached the gate, West stepped around the only tree left from the field it once had been. It was our tree, and although I couldn't get West to fess up, I knew he'd had something to do with it not being cut down. Our first kiss had been at the tree. It was very possible I had lost a piece of my heart the night West Ashby kissed me there and I hadn't even known his name.

He stopped in front of the tree and waited for me to get to him. The black shirt he was wearing fit his sculpted chest. He was beautiful, especially when he stood like that with his arms behind his back and his jean-clad legs slightly apart.

"Hey," I said when I reached him.

He simply smiled at me. Then glanced back at the tree. "Funny thing about this tree," he said.

"Oh, really? What's that?" I asked, amused by his teasing tone.

He turned to look back at me. "My world was falling apart, and I found an angel right here, leaning up against his tree. She saved me. Then she stole my heart."

Smiling, I took a step toward him, but he shook his head and I stopped. Then he went down, and it took me a moment to realize he was on one knee. I stood there staring at him as he tilted his head back and his gaze locked with mine.

"I've been planning on forever with you since I was eighteen years old," he said as he opened a small black box in his hand. "Not a day has gone by since then that I haven't wanted you to be my wife. I'll love you until the day I die. Nothing will ever change that. Please, Maggie, be my wife."

Tears were once again filling my eyes as I looked from the square-cut diamond to West's face. I had thought of this moment for years now. Knowing one day it would come. I couldn't imagine a world without West. But as much as I wanted to shout *yes*, I felt a lump in my throat blocking it.

I didn't want West to ask me to marry him because I was pregnant. The idea that he was doing this out of pressure made it all seem forced, and I never wanted this to be something he wasn't ready for. He could have asked me three years ago, and I would have said yes. But he had waited.

My gaze went back to the ring, and I wanted to slide it on my finger so badly. I wanted this more than I realized. But how could I?

"Maggie, I've had this ring for months," he told me. "I was waiting until we were here. I wanted to do this in the exact place it all began."

I sniffled. "Really?" I asked hopefully.

He grinned. "Yes. I'm down here because I want a life with you. I want you to have my last name. I want you beside me forever. This isn't happening because you're pregnant."

I let out a sob, then nodded my head, unable to say anything just yet.

West took the ring from the box and slid it onto my finger, then he stood up and cupped my face with both his hands. "You're gonna have to stop crying on me, baby. It's messing me up."

I smiled through my tears. "They're happy tears," I told him.

"They fucking better be," he said just before his mouth pressed against mine.

Everything else fell away. It was just us at our tree. Kissing once again.

BRADY AND RILEY

Ten months ago: Bryony's seventh birthday

CHAPTER ONE

BRADY

"Why are we stopping at Grammy's?" Bryony asked when I pulled into my mother's driveway. My dad's SUV was here. That was why we were stopping. This wasn't normal. My parents weren't enemies. Time had passed, and they got along well enough. I'd found a way to forgive him, but that didn't mean I trusted him.

He shouldn't be at this house. It was Mom's house. He may have lived here with us before, but he had chosen another path. This wasn't his home anymore. I glanced down at Bryony.

"Boone is here," she said then, recognizing his vehicle.

"Yeah, he is," I replied. I had never allowed him to have

her call him anything other than his name. There were times I wanted to call him Boone. Times I wanted to punish him by not calling him Dad.

"Are we here to see him?" she asked with obvious excitement in her voice. Dad was good with Bryony. She adored him. He told her stories and always gave her money that she thought I didn't know about when she saw him. At first I'd not wanted her to know him, but Riley had made me see how that wasn't healthy for me or Bryony.

"Not exactly," I told her. I didn't want her going inside with me, but I doubted I was going to be able to stop her from that. She loved both my parents, and she wouldn't understand my asking her to stay in the truck.

She didn't ask any more questions and opened the door to hop out and run for the house. I sighed, knowing this confrontation would be more difficult with her there. I would have to be careful what I said and what she heard. The kid was smart. She picked up on things I often wished she didn't. The older she got, the sharper she became.

"Come on, Daddy!" she called after me when she was at the front door. After flashing me her mother's smile, she opened the door and went inside without knocking. Which was what my mother expected. Bryony treated my parents just like she treated Riley's. There was no difference in her attentions or affections. She loved them equally. That humbled me almost as much as her calling me Daddy.

Bryony had been my mom's salvation during the hardest times of her life. When I had been falling in love with Riley, I'd had no idea what a large part her daughter, our daughter, would play in my life. Riley had given me more than I deserved. I had gotten the best damn package deal a man could get.

When I reached the house, I walked inside through the door, which Bryony had left open for me. My dad had picked Bryony up and was swinging her around in a circle while she laughed.

"How's my girl today? Are you ready for the big birthday party?" he asked her.

"YES!" she shouted happily.

"I got you the biggest present. You just wait and see," he told her.

I doubted that, since Riley and I were giving her the purple sparkly bicycle she'd been begging for since January.

"What is it?" she asked with excitement lighting up her eyes.

"You'll just have to wait a few more hours to see," he teased her. "But what about we go sneak one of the cookies Grammy is decorating for your party?"

Bryony hugged him tightly. "YAY!"

Finally, my dad shifted his gaze to me. "Hello, son,"

he said, still smiling as he set Bryony down and she went running toward the kitchen, where the smell of sugar cookies wafted. Mom was in charge of making the sunshine-, tower-, and number-eight-shaped cookies and decorating them for Bryony's birthday party this afternoon.

"Dad," I replied with a nod.

I wasn't normally so formal with him, but this was the first time I'd found him here. In this house. With my mother, since the divorce. He wasn't supposed to be here. The house he had bought for him and his second wife was still his home, even though she'd divorced him after just two years. He had been smart enough to have her sign a prenup. The house had remained his.

It was after the divorce that I'd been okay with Bryony visiting him at his home. I didn't want Bryony around the woman who had been the reason for my parents' divorce. Before that, I had required he go to Riley's parents' house to see her. But never here. I didn't want him here with Mom. She had survived. She was doing great. Mom's heartbreak was healed.

"Why are you here?" I asked once I heard Mom's voice when Bryony entered the kitchen. I didn't want either of them overhearing this conversation.

My dad raised his eyebrows as if this question surprised him.

"I did live here for longer than you've been alive," he replied, as if that gave him a right to be here.

"But you chose another life. This isn't your home anymore," I replied.

Dad sighed as if I were being an unreasonable child. "Brady, your mom and I spent most of our lives together. We built this house together. We raised you in this house. We have a history."

"That you ruined with your selfish choices," I said.

The scowl on his face pissed me off. As if he had any right to defend himself. I had forgiven him, but I would never forget. That would be impossible.

"Things change. Time changes things. We all make mistakes. Your mother has—"

"I don't give a fuck if mom has forgiven you. I was there when she was broken and falling apart. Me, dad. ME! I was eighteen years old, and overnight I became a man. You forced me to become one. You gave me no choice. Mom needed me, and I was there. You weren't. Just because time has passed and I have forgiven you, and she has forgiven you, doesn't erase it. You cheated on her. You destroyed this family, and I was the one who held on. That little girl in there was the one who put it back together. She gave Mom a reason to smile. She did for her what I couldn't do. So I'm going to ask you again. Why are you here?"

Dad didn't say anything for a moment, and during the silence my thoughts went down several different paths, all of them leading me to showing him his way out and threatening him if he ever came back.

"You're right. About all of that. I know what I did, and not a day passes I don't regret it. But your mother is the only person on this earth who knows me. Who understands me. This isn't the first time I've been here. It's just the first time you've caught me here. I'm not leaving because you don't want me here. I will only leave if your mother tells me to."

The anger simmering in my veins felt as if it was going to explode.

"Brady." Mom's overly chipper tone instantly stalled my temper, and I inhaled deeply, hoping it would calm me down.

"Hey, Mom," I said, walking over to pull her into a hug. She smelled like vanilla, and for a moment all was okay. This wasn't a fucked-up mess.

"Do you need to leave Bryony with us and go help Riley set up the party?" she asked me.

I had been on my way to pick up the helium tank for the balloons when I had stopped here because of Dad's vehicle. I shook my head. "No, I just stopped by . . ." Pausing, I looked at Dad.

Mom understood without my having to say anything more.

She squeezed my arms and gave me a reassuring smile. "I see," she said. "Well, thank you for checking in on me. The cookies are coming along beautifully. Your father and I are going to bring them along with Bryony's presents in about an hour. I want to be there for Riley if she needs help."

"Mom," I said, not liking the fact she had put her and dad in a sentence together. "Let me come pick you up. I'm sure Dad has other places he needs to be."

"Brady," she pleaded softly. "This isn't something you would understand."

She was fucking right I didn't understand. I didn't understand at all.

"Can I lick the bowl, Grammy?" Bryony asked as she entered the room.

"Only if you share with me," Dad told her, making her giggle.

Mom glanced at my dad and Bryony, then back at me. "Some things in life don't make sense. But life happens, and we make our own choices. You can't make mine for me," she whispered.

Feeling as if she had just punched me in the stomach, I managed to nod. "Bryony," I said, looking over at my daughter. "You ready to go? Mommy needs my help."

"But I wanted to lick the bowl," she said, looking deflated.

"Leave her with us. We'll get her to the party on time," Mom said and reached up to pat my cheek as if I were five years old.

"Please, please, please, Daddy?" she begged. She was too young to be so good at manipulation. She knew exactly how to work me to get her way. The last thing I wanted was for her to get used to seeing my parents together. This wasn't a big, happy family. It was a broken one.

"Okay," I relented, unable to tell her and my mother no.

She beamed brightly at me then grabbed my dad's hand. "Let's go!" she told him then pulled him down the hallway toward the kitchen.

"Life happens, honey. One day you'll understand," Mom told me.

I shook my head. "No, Mom, I won't."

CHAPTER TWO

RILEY

"You need this table under the tent?" Nash asked me as I was putting cotton-candy-pink covers over the chairs, then tying them with purple bows.

I glanced back over my shoulder. "Yes, please, and can you hang these paper lanterns from the middle up there?" I asked, pointing to the center of the tent.

"Yup," he replied.

"Gunner! Get your ass in here. I need the ladder!" he called out.

I continued with the chairs, wondering why Brady wasn't here yet with the helium. Leaving Bryony with him was a bad idea. She'd probably talked him into stopping to get ice cream. That girl had him so tightly wound around her little finger it wasn't funny. He was going to have to learn to start telling her no.

"What the fuck you need a ladder for? It's a tent," Gunner called back.

"Gotta hang lanterns from the top of it," Nash replied.

"Lanterns?" he asked.

"Just bring it here," Nash yelled back at him.

Those two were comic relief. This was the third birthday of Bryony's that they had come to help set up. It had become tradition. It was three birthdays ago when Bryony had first called Gunner "Uncle Gunner." The way his face had looked in that moment had been priceless. He still got teased by Nash and Ryker for tearing up.

Bryony had no relationship with her biological father, and I doubted she ever would. But Gunner was her blood, and I had wanted her to know he wasn't just a friend of Brady's but her uncle. He was here because of her. Not Brady.

"Why are we hanging paper lanterns from the ceiling?" Gunner asked, staring up at the top of the tent with a frown.

"Because we were told to," Nash replied.

"What's the theme of this party again? Rumpel-stiltskin?" Gunner asked me.

I laughed out loud and shook my head. "No. Rapunzel," I told him.

"She was the one who ate the apple and went to sleep?" he asked.

"No, dumbass, that was Snow White. Even I know that," Nash said, shaking his head in disgust.

"Who the fuck's Rapunzel, then? Sounds like Rumpelstiltskin. Did they hook up?" Gunner asked me.

Still laughing, I shook my head and stood up from tying the last bow on the chairs. "No. That's not even Disney."

"Disney? I thought you said Rapunzel? Where's the mouse ears?"

"God, I hope you have a girl one day," Nash said, chuckling.

"Don't wish that shit on me," Gunner shot back at him.

The world as we know it would change if Gunner Lawton ever had a daughter. I walked over to the table Nash had brought under the tent to start to set it up when Mom walked out of the back door holding a tray with drinks and snacks.

"Brady just pulled up," she told me.

"Finally," I said, relieved that he could get the balloons blown up now.

"You boys need some nourishment?" Mom asked, and both guys dropped their lanterns and went to get what my mother had brought out as if they were starving. We had only been at this for two hours. I rolled my eyes and started working on decorating the table that would be for drinks. The fountain I had bought off Amazon was going to have edible glitter in the purple-colored apple juice coming down out of it. I couldn't wait for Bryony to see it.

"Sorry I'm late," Brady said behind me, then placed a kiss on my cheek.

"What did Bryony convince you to do?" I asked him, turning around to face him.

He frowned. "Nothing. Well, except to stay at Mom's and come with her . . . and my dad."

The way his tone dropped when he said "my dad" had me searching his face. He was upset. Worried and stressed. It was clearly etched all over his handsome features. I reached up and touched his arm.

"Your dad is coming with your mom?" I asked him to clarify I was understanding his mood.

He nodded. "He was at her house. I saw his SUV and stopped. That's why I'm late."

I wrapped my arms around him. There wasn't much I could say to make this any better. I knew all too well how badly his father's affair had affected him. He had come a long way since then, forgiving his dad and moving on from what he'd done. But I knew he'd never expected this. Not after all his mom had gone through.

"I'm good," he said and kissed the top of my head.

"Today isn't about that shit. It's about Bryony, and I have balloons to get blown up." He stopped and looked up at the ceiling. "You need me to hang the lanterns first?" he asked.

"No, Gunner and Nash are doing that," I assured him.

He glanced over at them eating the snacks Mom had brought out. "Yeah, they look hard at work," he drawled.

"They'll get it done," I told him, then stood on my tiptoes to kiss his stubbled jawline. "I like this on you," I whispered. "It's rugged."

His eyes swung back to me. "Rugged, huh?" he asked, his gaze no longer troubled.

I nodded.

"Does 'rugged' lead to me getting you naked?"

I laughed then. "Always."

He growled as he leaned down and captured my lips with his. My hands slid into his hair as he stepped closer to me. The mint taste of his gum was all the refreshment I needed.

"Jesus! We got a party to decorate for. Stop eating each other alive," Gunner called out, and Brady slowly moved back, breaking the kiss.

"He's a jackass. Tell me again why he's here," he said.

"Because he's your friend and Bryony's uncle," I reminded him.

He sighed and rolled his eyes. "Damn luck."

Laughing, I slapped his arm. "He's right. We need to get this finished up."

Brady nodded, then kissed me one more time quickly before turning to unbox the helium tank. I watched him for a moment, enjoying the view of his butt in those jeans. His T-shirt was just snug enough so I could see his muscles underneath. Smiling, I finally turned my attention back to the table and continued decorating. I could ogle my man later.

CHAPTER THREE

BRADY

The last of the twinkling lights had been secured to the tent, and the lanterns' battery-operated lights had been turned on. Riley had managed to create a fucking fairy tale in her parents' backyard. She was inside now getting changed for the party, and Nash had gone to help himself to the adult drink table. Gunner had left to go pick up Willa already, and I was the only one left out here. With their help, we had pulled this together in enough time to take a moment before the guests showed up.

"OH MY GOSH!!!" Bryony's squeal filled the back-yard, and I turned to see her running through the back gate with her eyes wide in disbelief. She ran past me and looked up at the lanterns and twinkling lights, then her gaze fell to the sparkly drink fountain thing that Riley had set up. "Daddy! Do you see this! It's, it's magical!"

Smiling, I understood why Riley went to all this trouble. Getting to experience Bryony so excited and amazed was worth every damn minute put into preparing for this two-hour party.

"Your momma is definitely magical," I agreed.

She spun around with her arms out, smiling brightly. "This is the most beautiful birthday party ever," she said, then ran over to hug my legs.

I ruffled her hair. "I agree. But you better go on inside and get dressed. The princess needs to have her proper party dress on before guests arrive," I told her.

She nodded, then skipped her way to the back door of the house.

"Oh, Brady!" Mom gushed as she entered the backyard. She was carrying a tray of cookies, and my father, who walked out behind her, was also carrying a tray. I took a deep breath and tried not to let it get to me.

"Riley's good at this. Like most all things," I said, then went over to take the tray from her hands. "These are fantastic, Mom," I told her.

She was still looking at everything. "I hope so. I wanted them to be worthy of this party, but I don't know if they are."

"They are a perfect addition. The kids are going to love them," I assured her, then walked over to put them out on the table with the other sweets. I knew Riley wanted to put them on the tiered tray she had, but I also knew she would want to do it a certain way. I didn't try and help with that.

"Better than anything we ever put together for you," Dad said, placing the other tray of cookies on the table.

"I was good with the campouts," I replied for Mom's sake, not his. He had been the one to take me and my friends camping for my birthdays. I had great memories of that time. I didn't want him taking that from me. But seeing him with Mom was making me hate him.

"They were all you'd talk about for months," Mom said, smiling. "Having a boy was easier than a girl. This is a lot more work than those camping trips."

"Riley loves doing it as much as Bryony loves having it," I told her.

"She's a wonderful mother," Mom said. She wanted to say more, and I didn't need to ask her to know what it was. Mom was ready for us to be married. She'd hinted about it for over a year now. It wasn't something Riley ever mentioned though, which was a relief. Our life was perfect and in my head marriage wasn't. Thinking about it too much terrified me but then when I looked at Riley I knew I'd never hurt her. It was an internal struggle I had been facing for awhile.

"Yes, she is," I agreed.

"Hey, Boone," Nash called out. "Come get a drink."

Dad nodded and touched Mom's back briefly before walking over to the adult refreshment table. I didn't miss it, and my hands clenched in fists at my sides as he walked away.

"Honey, please," Mom whispered. "Don't do this."

I shifted my glare from my father's back to my mother, then immediately softened as I saw her pleading eyes. "He can't be trusted, Mom."

She sighed and reached out to take my hand. "That isn't your decision to make. I've never stopped loving your father. Even when he . . . when it all happened. I couldn't shut the love off. We share a history. We share you. That doesn't just go away, son. He made a mistake, and I've forgiven him, but I won't ever be able to forget it. That will always be something that changed me. Changed us. Things will never be the same. But he learned something from all of that. And we are getting older. Life goes faster every day."

"But you don't have to settle for him. You're still young, Mom. You can have a life with someone who cherishes you."

"But I want a life with someone I love. Someone I have

loved the majority of my life. I want a life with your dad. I know you don't understand it, and I can't make you. But this is my choice. I fought it. I won't lie to you. I wanted to hate him. I wanted to move on. But I couldn't. He's always going to be my one."

Sighing in frustration, I ran a hand through my hair. How can she feel like this? Why? Why can't she let him go and find a man who is worthy of her?

"Put yourself in my shoes. Twenty years from now, with the stress of life, work, and family all getting in the way of being a partner. Remembering to spend time together. To work on your marriage because you have too many other things getting in the way. You find out that the woman you've loved and built a life with has cheated on you. Could you stop loving her? Could you walk away and never look back?"

I opened my mouth to say that it wasn't the same, but I stopped. Because I had no fucking idea what that was like. I hadn't experienced that life yet. I stared at my mom and thought about Riley. The realization that nothing on this earth could make me stop loving her sank in. She couldn't change that. No matter what she did to me, I couldn't stop loving her and wanting her. I would forgive her for anything. It was something I didn't understand about Nash. How he was staying away from Tallulah when it was clear he was empty inside. He needed her, so why couldn't he forgive her?

I turned my head to look at my father, who was laughing at something Nash was saying. My dad seemed happy. It had been years since I'd seen him truly happy. He didn't appear as uptight and stressed as I once remembered. His gaze moved to Mom, and there was a softness in his eyes as he looked at her.

Fuck.

Damn.

Shit.

I didn't want to understand this. I didn't want my mom hurt again. I didn't trust that man, but what did I know? I was twenty-four years old. There was a diamond ring hidden under the seat of my truck and had been for six months. I wanted Riley forever, more than I wanted my next breath, but I hadn't asked her to marry me. I'd had plenty of chances, but my fear of marriage had held me back. It was my dad's fault I was so damn scared of it. When I knew Riley and Bryony should have my last name. That they were mine just as much as I was theirs. We were a family and yet I couldn't bring myself to make it legal.

As I stood there thinking about Mom's words and watching my parents look at each other as if they were twenty-four, I thought about them. They were why marriage scared the shit out of me. Deep down, I was terrified of hurting Riley, of becoming my father. I was scared of myself.

The fact is I'd lived through my mother's pain. I had held her when she had cried. The devastation my father had caused was so deeply ingrained in me, there was no fucking way I'd ever do that to Riley. I could never want anyone but her. Even when the bills were past due, and the kids were all screaming, and I hadn't gotten her to myself for weeks. I would just want her. Only her. Even if it was the moment I got to hold her in the morning before I left for work. It would just be her.

The thing I hadn't considered while I struggled with fear of marriage was that I wasn't weak like my dad.

I was strong like my mother. I loved the way she loved. Unconditionally. Just because I was a man didn't mean I was a product of my father. My mother's love had taught me more than he ever had. I was the man she had raised me to be. Not the man my father had been.

CHAPTER FOUR

RILEY

Pink icing smeared across the smile on Bryony's face as she raced by me toward the inflatable slide and jump house my parents had rented made this all worth it. Her laughter filled the backyard and she turned to grab her friend Amy's hand as they climbed into the jump house in their princess dresses.

Two hours had passed, but the party was still going. Adults were enjoying the cocktails I had made while the kids were still working out all the sugar they'd consumed. My baby was seven years old. I'd been so busy today, I hadn't let that sink in. How had seven years come and gone so quickly?

When they'd placed her in my arms, I'd been so terrified. I had been a kid myself, but one little look from her sweet face and I'd known I would move heaven and earth for her. I had no regrets. Not one. I would go through it all over again to have her. She was a gift that had turned a nightmare into something else.

Brady walked across the lawn toward the inflatable and waited for Bryony to come down the slide. I watched him, feeling my heart squeeze as he laughed at her sliding down sideways. She beamed up at him and threw her arms around his neck. I loved that man. More than I'd ever thought possible. Every moment I watched him be the dad to Bryony that I'd never thought she'd have, I loved him more. So much, my heart felt like it would explode at times. Although he hadn't asked me to marry him, we were a family already. We didn't need a marriage license to make us one. I knew that deep down Brady struggled with marriage because of what he went through with his parents. I understood that and having his love was enough.

He whispered something to Bryony, and she nodded, then took his hand, and they walked toward the house. I studied them, wondering if he had a present he hadn't told me about for her. We had already given her the bike she'd wanted so badly. Although Boone's gift had been a close second. The newest Barbie Dreamhouse, complete with a garage and Tesla, was a massive hit with her too. It was also far more expensive than her bike had been.

I started to walk toward the door to see what they were up to in there when my mom called out my name. I turned to see her at the punch fountain. "We need more purple shiny juice," she told me. "The kids are getting thirsty again."

I walked over to her and reached under the table to find the bottle of apple juice I had in a cooler. I had already put the purple food coloring in it, along with the edible glitter. "We just add this," I told her.

"Why didn't we get sparkly drinks?" Gunner asked.

"You can always drink the fancy apple juice," I told him.

He looked as if he were considering it. "I'll stick with the whiskey."

Laughing, I shook my head and turned to check the adult beverage table to make sure it didn't need restocking. The party didn't seem to be winding down.

I realized the Disney playlist that Bryony had chosen had stopped playing, and I started out of the tent to go restart the computer. It had probably gone through all thirty songs again. Just as I made it halfway across the yard, Taylor Swift's "Love Story" started playing, and I paused. Bryony loved that song, along with everything else Taylor sang. Had she changed the playlist?

The back door opened then, and Bryony came out doing the choreographed dance she had taught Brady weeks ago. They did it to many songs at the house. She thought it was funny to get him to dance, and he had a hard time telling her no. Once she batted her eyes at him and begged, he always gave in.

I stopped and watched her, highly entertained by her performance. When Brady then followed her out the door and began doing the same dance, a burst of laughter came from me as well as some hoots and cheers from the guests behind me.

Crossing my arms over my chest, I watched as the two people I loved most in the world sang along to "Love Story" and danced. Unable to stop the grin on my face. Brady swore he would never do this dance in public, but here he was making Bryony's birthday party epic. That man would do anything for her. One day she would realize how incredibly lucky she was.

When Bryony reached me, she stopped and sang, "It's a love story, baby, just say *yes*," with a huge grin on her face, then stepped back, and Brady stopped in front of me.

In that moment, it was if time had stilled. Everything and everyone around us had faded away as I watched Brady go down on one knee. I heard Bryony's squeal of delight, but all I could see was him. Looking up at me. His crooked grin and then the small ring box he opened in his hand with the most beautiful diamond I had ever seen.

"This is forever," he said. "It'll always just be you . . . Marry me?"

I let out a sob, then covered my mouth as tears started streaming down my face. I managed to nod, then blurted out, "Yes!"

Bryony threw her arms around my legs, and the clapping, whistles, and cheering filled the backyard.

"We did it, Daddy! She said yes!" Bryony's excitement made me cry even harder. "And I get to be a Higgens too, Mommy! Daddy said he wants me to be a Higgens too!"

The sobs came harder as Brady stood up and pulled me into his arms, then slid the ring onto my finger. I could hardly see it through my tears, but what it looked like wasn't important. I would have happily worn a string on my finger if he had put it there.

Brady cupped my face and wiped away my tears with his thumbs, then pressed a kiss to my lips. "Always, Riley. You and Bryony have been my forever since the day you climbed into my truck to get out of the rain. I just didn't know how damn lucky I was. But I swear to you I will never forget."

"This is the best day ever!" Bryony said.

Brady bent down and picked her up, then pulled me to

his other side. "It's not every day the two most beautiful women in the world agree to be mine," Brady told her.

There just wasn't enough room in my chest to hold the love I felt in that moment. I'd never imagined I would have this. Once I had thought my dad would have to be Bryony's father figure. I hadn't thought I would find a man that I trusted to love her enough. To want her, too.

But I hadn't been expecting Brady Higgens either. Of all the boys in Lawton, I'd managed to win the love of the best one. My fairy tale had come true.

GUNNER AND WILLA

"This was going to be a journey, but it was one she had needed for far too long."

CHAPTER ONE

WILLA

Nonna put a cup of coffee and a slice of pie in front of me on the table. I had mentioned missing her apple pie last month when we talked on the phone, and she'd remembered. This one was still warm from the oven, and the smell had been the first thing that hit me when I walked in the door.

"This is heaven," I said with a sigh of happiness.

"If you and Gunner would have stayed here while visiting, you'd have had that and more by now," Nonna said with a smug smile on her face.

I felt guilty about that, but staying at Nash's had been something Gunner wanted to do for this visit. This was the end of the field party and the beginning of something new.

I was proud of Ryker and Nash for all they had done and were going to do.

"I know, Nonna. But we always stay here. This is a big deal for the guys, and being there among them through this was something Gunner wanted to do."

Nonna nodded. "I understand that. I'm just pointing out the facts. I baked two pies and a batch of brownies for you to take over to the Lee boy's house. But you tell Gunner I still expect him to come see me again. He's only stopped by the one time this trip, when y'all first arrived."

"He will, Nonna," I assured her.

She poured herself a cup of coffee, then took the chair across from me. "I've got some things to talk to you about. Ain't something I'm wanting to do, but it's got to be done."

I put my fork back down without taking the bite of pie from it. When Nonna made that face, it was never a good thing. Although I wasn't a kid anymore, that expression and tone of voice made me feel ten.

"What is it?" I asked, watching her closely.

She sighed heavily and gripped her coffee cup in her arthritic hands.

"Nonna, are you sick? Is something wrong?" I asked, feeling panic grip me.

She shook her head. "No, it ain't me. It's your mom."

Relief and unease settled over me then. Nonna was fine.

I could live with that. As for my mother, we didn't speak of her. Even my brother, Chance, never mentioned her when we spoke or visited. He did talk about Bella, our six-year-old little sister, who I had never met. He adored her, and I knew he wanted me to know her. If it weren't for my mother, I would want to also. But seeing Bella meant seeing my mother.

"Oh" was all I could manage as a response.

"She's got the cancer, and it ain't good," Nonna told me. I could see the pain in her eyes, and that hurt me more than anything. I knew how much my nonna loved my mother, even if it was one-sided. My mother only loved herself.

"I'm sorry, Nonna," I said.

She nodded. "I reckon I didn't expect much more of a reaction from you, but that isn't what this is about."

I waited for her to continue without saying anything. Part of me felt guilty for not reacting with more emotion but then if anyone would understand my relationship with my mother it was Nonna.

"Chance is still a kid himself. You know that. He stayed with your momma for Bella's sake when his dad left. He's been protecting Bella and taking care of her. She ain't any better a momma to that little girl than she was to you. Except you didn't have a big brother to step in and save you."

"She also has her dad. He adores Chance. I can't imagine Rick feels any differently about Bella." I could hear the bitterness in my tone. After all these years, I still disliked the man. He'd never wanted me in their home. He treated me as if I were an outsider to their little family. Chance never talked about his father to me. He knew how I felt about him. Chance wasn't a kid anymore. He was old enough to drink, but I didn't point that out to Nonna.

"Rick ran off with some young woman two years ago, Willa. Chance hasn't heard from him but once since then. He was living in some town in Oklahoma, but Chance doesn't know the address, and he don't have a good number for him no more."

I'd had no idea, but then Chance would never tell me things like this. I felt guilty for making my brother feel like he couldn't share this with me. My dislike of the man shouldn't override my brother's problems. He should be able to talk to me. I was his big sister. It was my job to be there for him no matter what. Even if we had grown up with very different situations.

"I didn't know," I said simply.

Nonna gave me a sharp look. "Because your brother said it wasn't your problem and not to bother you with it."

My brother sounded a lot more grown-up than Nonna was giving him credit for but he also trying to take on too much. I was going to tell him just that as soon as I spoke with him.

"Is that why he didn't tell me about Mother?" I asked, wanting this to make some sort of sense. I had never acted as if his problems weren't important. I'd always tried to be there for him. He had just never seemed to truly need me. He had the family I was born into that hadn't wanted me. They had wanted him, or at least I had thought they had.

She shook her head. "No. I told her and him both that I'd tell you."

"So, what's the deal? Is she going to get chemotherapy? Is she asking you to take Bella in?" I didn't think my nonna was still able to raise kids. She needed to enjoy her life and retirement. Gunner had given her enough money when he sold the Lawton estate that she would never need to work again. Her world revolved around playing bingo at the church on Friday nights, walking three miles every day with her friends, and working at the soup kitchen and the ladies' auxiliary at her church to supply clothing for those in need. This was not the time in her life she needed a six-year-old girl to raise.

"Chemotherapy isn't an option. It's everywhere, Willa. She's beyond saving. She skipped several years of doctor checkups, and it's spread all through her. They say she has about six months if she's lucky. Three if she's not."

Nonna's words slowly sank in as I sat there staring down at my slice of pie. There was no real emotion that I understood running through me at the moment. I hadn't seen my mother since she'd stood in this house and told me she was pregnant and I was useless. We hadn't spoken since that day either. I had hated her for so long for not loving me, until one day the hate changed to indifference. I rarely thought of her anymore.

Tears didn't sting my eyes at the news she was going to die. My chest didn't ache, and there were no regrets. Shouldn't I feel at least one of those things? Anything? Was I truly that cold and switched off from the woman who gave birth to me?

"She's not got much in her will to leave to anyone, but unless Rick shows back up, she is leaving Bella in Chance's custody. She knows I'm too old to raise another kid, and I barely know the child. I've only gotten to know Chance since he turned sixteen and made it a point to come see me. His visits are something I look forward to. I hate I missed his earlier years, but your mother is to blame for that. She did give me you, though, and you are my greatest joy."

At those last four words, a lump did form in my throat. My nonna had loved me enough to make up for not having the love of either parent. She had been my mother and my father. She had been my lifeline and protector. Oddly enough, she had been that for Gunner, too. She loved him like her own.

"He's too young to raise a kid," I managed to say.

Nonna sighed wearily. "I said the same thing, but Chance is set on it. He won't hear of anything else. You've lived with your mother, Willa. You know what it is like. Chance has been that child's everything since she was old enough to walk. He's the one who made sure she was fed properly, he's the one who got her ready for school and took her to school, he's the one who holds her when she's hurt. He's been her parent since he was fifteen years old."

My chest hurt thinking about it. Deep down had I known all this, but it was something I had chosen to ignore. That wasn't my world. It never really had been. Even when I lived in that house, I wasn't part of the family. But Chance was my family and ignoring his reality had been wrong. Had I truly believed that his life was different with our mother or had I wanted to believe he was fine? That the sister I had never met was loved? Facing the truth was more than a slap in the face. It felt more like a heavy weight had been placed on my chest and I couldn't take a deep breath.

CHAPTER TWO

GUNNER

Nash looked up from the paperwork on the kitchen table in front of him when I walked inside his house. He ran a hand over his head and groaned. "Thank God for a distraction," he said.

I looked down at the papers in front of him. "Looks fun."

"It's applications for the camp," he replied. "This shit ain't easy. I want to take them all."

"Is Willa back yet?"

He shook his head. "No."

I walked over to the fridge and got a bottle of water before going to sit down across from Nash. "She's visiting her nonna. I figured I'd give them a visit without me. They don't get that often," I said, then took a long pull from my water.

"Where have you been?" he asked.

I thought for a moment. I wasn't sure I was ready to tell anyone what I had been doing. It was something I had a hard time believing myself. I lifted my gaze from the water bottle in my hand to meet Nash's curious expression.

"You wouldn't believe me if I told you," I said with a smirk.

"Now you *have* to fucking tell me," he replied.

"No one knows about this, and I don't want them to. Not until I tell Willa."

He nodded. "My lips are sealed. Spill."

"Not even Tallulah," I added. "The girls can't keep secrets from each other. They do too much chatty shit."

"Not even her," he agreed.

"I just made an offer on the estate," I told him.

His eyebrows drew together. "The Lawton estate? The place you sold?"

I nodded. "Yep."

Nash leaned back in his chair and let out a long, low whistle. "Holy shit," he murmured; then a smile spread across his lips. "You're fucking coming home."

I shrugged and took another drink of my water.

Nash laughed out loud. "Damn, this is good news. First Asa and now you."

"It's home for both me and Willa. I tried running from it, thinking I'd find somewhere else that worked for us, but this is home. Willa misses her nonna and worries about her. Hell, I do too. The woman can cook. Bryony is the only blood relative I have that I care about. I want to be in her life. She's growing so fucking fast."

"And then there is me," Nash added, still grinning.

"Sure, keep telling yourself that," I drawled.

"So you think Willa is going to want this? The Lawton Estate? Moving back without talking to her?" Nash asked.

I nodded. "Yeah, she is. It's not something she brings up a lot but when she talks about the future she mentions moving back here. Taking care of her nonna. Being home. I think this is ultimately where she wants us to be but she won't tell me that. She thinks I am happy with our current plans."

He slapped his hand on the table and stood up. "This calls for a celebration. Let's day drink."

"They haven't accepted my offer yet. The place wasn't on the market," I told him. When we had driven into town and Willa's eyes filled with emotion as she sighed and said "We're home." I'd decided then to make an offer on the Lawton estate. If this place made her that happy, then it was what I wanted too.

He cut his eyes back at me. "Yeah, but you offered them enough to make them want to sell."

I shrugged. "Possibly."

"That's my obnoxious, rich, yet loveable Gunner. I'm getting us a beer," he said just as the front door opened and Tallulah walked in with a tray of goodies that I knew were straight from her momma's kitchen.

"Beer at noon? Really?" she asked, looking at Nash.

He paused and then smiled at her. "Maybe not this early," he replied.

She smirked and put the tray on the table. "Milk goes better with these caramel fudge cookies than beer anyway," she told him then looked over at me. "Is Willa here? I need to find shoes for the field dedication. I was hoping she could help me shop."

I started to shake my head when there was a knock this time on the door before it opened up. Willa stepped inside, and she didn't have to speak for me to know something was wrong. Her gaze swung to mine, and the look in her eyes had me standing up and forgetting about the cookies.

"Hey," I said, walking toward her. "What's wrong?"

She shook her head and forced a smile. "It's fine," she replied, placing her hand on my arm.

"No, it's not. You can't lie to me," I told her.

She sighed, and her shoulders slumped. "Not right

now, okay?" she said, then looked at the other two over my shoulder. "Oh! I have pies and brownies in the car. I forgot them. Nonna sent them."

"I'll get them, but walk with me," I said, placing my hand on her back and turning around toward the door.

She didn't argue, thankfully. I wasn't waiting to find out why she looked so damn upset. I was hoping to give her good news later today. This was not how I wanted her to be when that happened.

"Talk, baby," I said the moment the door closed behind us.

She took a few more steps, then turned to look up at me. "My mother has cancer. She's dying. Six months if she's lucky," she said without taking a breath. "And I . . . I don't know if I care and if that makes me a bad person or if it's okay to feel nothing."

I pulled her into my arms and held her against my chest. Her mother was a fucking piece of shit. I hated the woman more than I hated my own mother, and that was saying a lot. But it was clear Willa was feeling something. Her eyes never lied.

"Is it that you feel something and you don't want to maybe?"

She shook her head against my chest. "No. I'm upset for Nonna. I'm worried about Chance, who is going to be twenty-one raising a six-year-old little girl. Rick ran off a few years ago, apparently. Yet Chance has told me nothing. He has kept so much a secret from me and I have let him. I'm his sister and I should have known. And I am worried about my soul because I feel nothing for her. I don't feel any emotion for my mother at all. Just for those this will affect."

Damn. I sighed and pressed my lips to the top of her head. Her visit with Ms. Ames hadn't been a lighthearted one. I regretted not going now. She had needed me for all this. I wish I'd been told before so I could have been there.

"I'm sorry," I said to her as she leaned heavier against my chest and clung to me.

"You don't think I'm broken, do you? Because I can't love her or feel something?"

"Fuck no. She killed anything you could have felt for her years ago. She was never your mother, Willa. Nonna is your mother. She's what a mother is, not that woman. She just gave birth to you."

Willa nodded, her head against my chest. "That's what I keep telling myself. But my heart is heavy. For Chance especially. He never told me about his dad leaving and that Mother didn't take care of Bella. I didn't know all that. I knew he adored Bella, but Chance loves big. It's his thing. I missed a lot from our visits and phone calls. I ignored it.

He had no one, and I didn't know. I should have known. I should have checked. I should have put my feelings for my mother aside and gotten to know my sister. If I had, then I would have known the other stuff."

I barely knew her brother. She saw him maybe twice a year, and I'd only been with them three times. They normally met up and spent time just the two of them. I thought it was what she wanted and they needed. As for the little sister, not even Willa knew her. She did send presents to Bella for her birthday and Christmas, but that was all. I had wondered if one day she would regret the time she lost with her and now I felt as if I should have said something. Seeing her like this was breaking my heart.

"Chance did what he thought he should do. He knew bringing you into the situation wouldn't help anything. That woman would say the wrong thing to you and I'd have had to shut her up. It would have gotten ugly."

Willa let out a small laugh as she sighed. "Maybe, but he needed me. My brother needed me and I did nothng."

"First of all, there's no 'maybe' to it. If she'd have lashed out at you with her nasty mouth, I'd have shut it for her. No one talks to you that way. I don't give a fuck who they are. And second, you love your brother and he knows that. He also understands why you are the way you are about your mother."

Willa tilted her head back to look up at me. "You realize you can't protect me from the world."

I scowled. "The fuck I can't!" I replied, annoyed. Because yes, I could, and I was going to spend the rest of our lives doing just that.

She smiled then. "I love you. You're crazy, but I love you."

Hearing her say those words while she gazed up at me with eyes that reflected how she felt made my world right. It warmed me and reminded me how damn lucky I was.

"I hear crazy love is the best kind," I replied.

She nodded. "Definitely."

CHAPTER THREE

WILLA

"There's something else," I told Gunner as we walked back toward the house with the treats Nonna had sent with me.

"What?" he asked, stopping to look down at me.

"Chance is coming today. He should be at Nonna's by five. He's . . . he's bringing Bella." That was what I knew was making me emotional. Every time I thought about seeing the sister I had never met and had only seen pictures of, it did something to my chest. I wanted to see her, but after all these years it was also terrifying. Then there was the guilt that had set in for not knowing she was being treated the same way I had been by our mother.

"I'm going with you," Gunner said.

I nodded. "Yes, I want you to," I assured him. He had looked ready to argue with me.

He relaxed a little then. "You're scared."

"Yeah, I am," I admitted. "And regretful, angry at myself."

"Why?"

I shook my head and then shrugged. I had explained all this to him. Just because he didn't agree did not make me feel it any less. He shifted the food in his hands to one arm and took my chin between his two fingers.

"Bella is not your mother. She's a little girl. One who has heard nothing but good things about you from Chance. She'll love you, Willa. Don't let the shit your mother has put in your head mess with you."

I felt my eyes well up with tears. How was it Gunner could put what I was feeling it into words for me even when I couldn't.

"You think?" I asked him, my voice raspy with emotion. Would she blame me for not being there? How could he be sure she wouldn't?

"I fucking know," he said, leaning so that his face was only inches from mine. "You're so damn easy to love."

I smiled then. "Says my boyfriend."

He smirked. "Says the man who has loved you since he was a kid."

"Which means you're a little biased," I replied.

"No, baby. I don't love easy. You know that."

I nodded. He was definitely a hard one to crack. His life had made him difficult to get close to. He protected himself at all costs. Somehow I was the exception.

"Come on, they're waiting on us, and I know you want to eat whatever Tallulah's mother has sent and some of this pie," I told him.

He studied me a moment. "You sure you're up to talking to anyone? And Tallulah is wanting you to go shoe shopping with her."

I thought about it for a moment. My head wasn't in the place to shop right now. I needed to be near Gunner. He made things easier to handle and accept.

"As long as I'm with you, I'll be fine."

"Are you saying I gotta shop for shoes?"

I laughed at the horror on his face. "No. I mean I can go inside and visit. I just don't want to go shopping. I want to be near you today."

A smile slowly spread across his face. It was territorial in a way. Gunner liked that I wanted him. He had very little to none of that from his family growing up. I filled a large gaping hole inside of him, and I knew it. That's why when he went all possessive of me, I handled it fine. I understood its source.

We walked back inside, and Tallulah stepped out of Nash's arms, breaking their kiss as if she had been caught doing something naughty. It was good to see them back together. When they had been broken up, it had felt like something was missing. Nash had been lost without her too.

"Please continue to suck face. Don't mind us," Gunner drawled.

"Hush," I told him, still grinning.

Tallulah laughed and pressed her fingers to her lips as she looked at Nash. He was a different man with her in his life. The twinkle in his eyes was back.

Gunner put Nonna's pies and brownies on the table, then sat down, pulling me into his lap. I looked at him, confused. He shrugged. "You said you wanted to stay close to me today. I'm keeping you close."

"I didn't mean this," I told him.

He winked at me, making my stomach feel fluttery. "I did."

Shaking my head, I glanced over at Tallulah, who was watching me. "Are you okay?" she asked me.

I nodded. "Yeah, just family drama. More than I was ready to deal with."

She seemed to understand and walked over to take the cover off one of the pies. "This smells delicious," she said with a sigh.

"It is," I assured her.

"If I eat this I'll have to run three miles," she groaned, and Nash walked up behind her, taking her waist in his hands.

"If you think you need to burn calories, I have a better idea," he whispered, loud enough for us to hear.

"Nash!" she squealed as her cheeks turned bright pink and he leaned down to nibble her ear.

I looked away and reached for one of the chocolate cookies on the table, then took a bite. Gunner leaned over and sank his teeth into the cookie, then pulled it from my grasp.

"Nash! No," I heard Tallulah say and looked back over at them. Nash had her arm and was pulling her away from the table.

"Come on," he urged her, and I could see her body slowly caving in as she let him draw her to him and toward the door.

"Y'all keep that shit down in there. I'm eating," Gunner told them just as they reached the door to the kitchen.

"I make no promises," Nash called back as they disappeared through the doorway.

"Maybe we should go somewhere and give them some privacy," I suggested. "They just got back together after two years."

Gunner seemed to think about it for a moment then nodded. "Yeah, okay. Grab some of those cookies and brownies, though. I'll go get my keys."

I stood up and he grabbed my butt, making me squeal in surprise. "Damn, I love your ass."

I glanced back at him and smiled. "Good, because I'm about to eat a brownie, and I am not at all worried about the calories. There will be no running them off for me."

CHAPTER FOUR

GUNNER

Willa had been silent most of the way to her grandmother's house. I knew she was nervous. She had been so distracted all afternoon that when I got the call that the owners of the house that had once been mine accepted my offer, she hadn't questioned who I was talking on the phone or what it was about.

That had worked in my favor, but I didn't like seeing her so tensed up. I had taken her hand in mine to keep her from fidgeting with them. I thought maybe my touch would calm her, but so far that wasn't working. The closer we had gotten, the more tense she had grown.

When I pulled into the driveway, I parked the car, then

reached over and took her chin between my fingers to turn her face toward me. Her eyes were wide and so many emotions were on display I wanted to pull her into my arms and run off with her. Somewhere that nothing could hurt her or upset her. It wasn't rational, but that was what I wanted.

"I won't leave your side. If at any moment you need to get out, you take my hand and I will make our excuses. Everyone in there loves you. One just doesn't know it yet, but she will. Take a deep breath," I said, then leaned down and kissed her gently on the lips. "It'll all be fine. I swear."

She nodded and squeezed my hand. "You're right. It's time I start making up for not being there," she whispered. "Let's go."

I got out of the G-Wagon and walked over to her side to take her hand in mine. We walked to the front door just as it opened up and Chance stepped out. He and Willa shared the same smile. That had thrown me the first time I met him.

"God, I've missed you!" he said, coming down the stairs, and I let her hand go so she could go to her younger brother.

He enveloped her in a hug, towering over her and me. By the time he was seventeen he had been six feet, five inches. It was a shame he didn't care for basketball. He'd have been great at it.

I watched them hug tightly. Chance looked at me over her head and nodded with his friendly smile. "Good to see you too, Gunner. Looks like you're taking care of my sister."

"Always," I assured him.

The expression on his face told me he respected me for that alone.

"Is she here?" a small voice asked as a tiny blonde with a head full of wild curls stepped out onto the porch.

Chance looked down at the girl. "Bella, this is your sister, Willa. Willa, this is Bella."

The girl stared up at Willa, and I watched as Willa stepped closer to her, then squatted down to her level. "It's really nice to meet you, Bella. I've heard so much about you from Chance."

Bella gave her a small smile. "You don't look like her," she said as if she were relieved.

Willa glanced up at Chance, confused.

He cleared his throat and ruffled her blond curls. "I told you she didn't," he replied to the girl.

She smiled brighter then. "You smile pretty," she then told Willa.

"Thank you," Willa said. "So do you."

Bella seemed pleased with that. "Her smile isn't nice."

"Whose?" Willa asked, glancing at Chance again but I

could see the pain in her eyes. She knew and it was hurting her to think that Bella had suffered.

"Mother's," she replied.

I saw the glance that passed between Chance and Willa, and I knew there were more things that Willa didn't know. But even from here I was understanding it, so I knew Willa was too. She'd lived it. This was going to be hard on her. Much harder than I had realized. She was already beating herself up about not knowing. The more demons that came out of the closet, the more Willa would take it as her fault.

"Let's all go inside with Nonna," Chance said, breaking the sudden tension.

The girl looked past Willa to meet my gaze. "Who is he?" she asked.

Willa stood up and turned to me. "That's Gunner. He's my boyfriend," she told her, then held out her hand for me to come closer and take it.

"It's nice to meet you, Bella," I told her.

She gave me a shy smile, then ducked her head.

"He does that to most girls. It's that pretty face of his," Willa said, making Bella giggle.

Chance took Bella's hand and led her back inside. Willa leaned against me just enough for me to feel it but not enough to be obvious. Her hand squeezed mine, and I squeezed back. This was a lot for her, and now she had more to learn. It was clear Chance was holding back the complete truth. Willa needed me and I would be whatever she needed. I wasn't leaving her side. We would face whatever else was to come together.

Ms. Ames was putting food on the table, and the house smelled like fried chicken and biscuits. I'd loved both those things as a kid, and Ms. Ames made the best.

Her eyes lifted, and she met mine. "There's my other boy," she said, smiling. "Now y'all find a seat and let's eat. Best talking is done around the dinner table."

Willa moved to the table, and we took a seat while Bella kept her eyes on Willa as she chose the chair beside her. I glanced over at Chance, and the pleased look on his face said more than any words could. He had wanted his sisters to know each other. Their mother had done a lot of damage to all of them. Maybe more to the ones she'd kept.

"This looks amazing. Thank you, Nonna," Chance said as he took his seat across from me and beside his grandmother.

"No need to thank me. I've been cooking for these two since they were babies. I miss not getting to do the same for you and Bella. I have a lot of time to make up for," she told him, then patted his cheek before turning to Bella and asking her what she wanted to drink.

Willa stood up then. "Oh, let me help with the drinks," she said.

"Sit! You've got things to take in, and, well, I want you to sit. At least for tonight," Ms. Ames told her with a serious expression.

Willa sat back down slowly, and I squeezed her thigh, then left my hand there once she was seated beside me again. She had relaxed somewhat since we'd arrived. She turned her attention to Bella.

"Chance tells me you're a great student. He said you were reading before you were four years old. That's very impressive," Willa said to her.

Bella lit up at the compliment. "Chance taught me to read. I love books. They tell the best stories," she told Willa and glanced at me a moment to smile shyly.

Willa looked over at her brother. "He left out the part where he taught you to read."

Chance shrugged. "She was a fast learner. I realized she was trying to read everything from cereal boxes to magazines mother left lying around. So I went and got a library card, and we began getting books each week."

"The library is our favorite place. All the good things happen there," Bella said as if she was sharing a wonderful secret.

Willa placed her hand on mine under the table, and I turned my hand over so that I could thread my fingers through hers. This was going to be a journey, but it was one she had needed for far too long. I just feared the steps it took to get her through it. Pain was going to be involved and I hated to know she would hurt. I wanted to save her from everything. I always had. This time I couldn't but I would be there while she waded through.

CHAPTER FIVE

WILLA

Bella had kept us very entertained during dinner with stories about her school, Chance, and her friends. Not once did she mention our mother. When the topic went in any direction that Mother might be brought up, she would pause and go in another direction. She was way too wise for her years, and I knew that had a lot to do with the home life she had been given. Although Chance seemed to have done an excellent job taking care of her. The guilt that I hadn't been there to do the same for him and her weighed on me heavily.

Rick had always kept Chance by his side. They had gone to ball games together and played catch in the yard.

He had even taken Chance on trips with him that I didn't get to go on, and when Mother had to stay behind with me she resented me for it. Not once had I considered that my brother's life had been hard. That he had been neglected. If I had . . . I wouldn't have kept my distance. I wouldn't have let our mother keep us from being together. All three of us.

Sitting around the living room, Chance and Gunner were talking while Bella showed me every special item she had in her backpack. They ranged from shiny rocks she had found to tiny little dolls that Chance had bought her as rewards for good grades. I learned all about her best friend Mags and how they could swing the highest on the playground.

When Chance finally told Bella it was time for bed, she sulked only a moment, then hugged me tightly before going to do the same to Nonna. She paused at Gunner and ducked her head, unsure what to do, and he held out his arms. "Hey, I like hugs too," he told her.

That was all the encouragement she needed. She threw herself into his arms and gave him a hug before blushing as she called out good night to us all and then followed Chance to the bedroom that had been mine once.

I looked at Nonna as I fought back the emotion clogging my throat. I had made a mistake and I couldn't go back in time. I should have known my sister. Tonight, I was seeing all I had missed. Hearing about her life rather than being a part of it.

"Not sure how luck had it, but none of my grandchildren inherited their mother's meanness. I just don't know where I went wrong with that one. I shouldn't have let her daddy spoil her so." Nonna looked so sad in that moment I wanted to get up and wrap my arms around her, but she stood up before I could move. "You need to talk to Chance. I'm going to go clean up the kitchen."

Gunner stood up. "I'll help you," he told her, then looked down at me. "That is, if you don't need me." The concern in his gaze made me feel warm inside where I had been cold before. I always needed him. Especially now I was finding my strength from him but I couldn't lean on him to face this. It wasn't his fault.

I shook my head. "No, I'm fine."

He kissed my head and whispered that he loved me, then followed Nonna into the kitchen. I waited only a few minutes before Chance reappeared.

"They've gone to clean up the kitchen," I told him.

He let out a weary sigh and sank back down onto the sofa.

"So, talk to me. How are things? Is Mother being difficult? Does Bella know?" I wanted to apologize for not knowing. For not being there. For everything but I knew if

I did I would start to cry. I could barely keep from it now.

He massaged his temples a moment, then lifted his gaze to mine.

"When is Mother not difficult? And yes, Bella knows. Mother is very verbal about her death and using it to manipulate and lash out. You would think with death being near, she would change, but she's just gotten worse. I just couldn't keep Bella there any longer. I had to get her out. I've stayed in that house for Bella, but this morning I went and signed a lease on an apartment in Little Rock. It's located in Bella's school district, so she can keep going to her school. We are staying here two days to visit, then I am going back there to move Bella and me out of that house. I warned Mother last week if she couldn't speak with kindness to her daughter, then I would take her away and no court would stop me."

"Do you need money?" I asked him. I had to do something. He'd done it all for far too long. I wanted to offer more but my head was spinning with what it was I could possibly do.

He shook his head. "No, my job pays well. I may not have gotten to go to college, but that's not needed for all careers in this world. I'm good at what I do."

Chance had been working for the power company for the past two years. He was a hard worker and a fast learner. I was proud of him and all he'd accomplished.

"What about furniture? Could I at least buy Bella a bedroom set? Something girly like I never had?" I asked him.

He grinned. "She'd love that. Especially is she knew it was from you."

I wanted to do more but I didn't know how to or what that could be. I leaned forward and reached out to grab his hand. "I wasn't there for you. I didn't think you needed me. I thought they were good to you. She acted like she loved you. I was wrong, I am so sorry, Chance. I failed you. Both of you."

He shook his head and squeezed my hand. "I was fine. Dad was around for most of my life, and when he split I was so busy taking up the slack with Bella, Mother relied on me. She didn't give me any shit. She never treated me like she did you . . . but Bella . . . she treats Bella badly." His tone went dark when he said the words, and my heart ached more than I thought was possible.

"I should have taken her from there years ago, but I wasn't financially ready. I am now. I know she's dying, but she won't change. She won't stop spewing her venom. I can't sacrifice Bella's emotional well-being."

"You're doing the right thing," I assured him. "And I want to help in any way I can. If you need me for anything call me. Please," I begged him.

He nodded. "I will. She's as taken with you as I knew

she would be. She needed a mother and didn't get one. You got Nonna, and I wish she'd been given the same. Now that she's met you, she's going to want to see you more."

I was going to make sure that happened. He was right, Nonna had been my mom. She'd been what healed me. I could be there for Bella. I would love her unconditionally. She was young and I had years, a lifetime to make up for missing out on so much. For not being the sister she needed. For the pain she'd been through because of our mother.

"Good. I want to see her. I regret so much," I said, then sighed, looking back at him. "What happens with Mother, her house? Who is going to take her to the doctor?" I hated to ask this, but she was our mother, and she was dying. Even if she was evil, she wouldn't be able to do this alone. I didn't want to care but something deep inside did.

He shrugged. "I'm trying to figure that out. I have my hands full with work and being a parent to Bella. I thought maybe hospice would step in soon. Until then I can fit in time to stop by once a day."

"I'll hire a private nurse to stay with her," Gunner said, walking back into the room.

Chance shook his head. "I can't let you do that. This isn't your problem."

"That's where you're wrong. Something affects Willa and Ms. Ames, then it is my problem. They're my family too."

Chance looked at me, and I nodded my head at him to accept. My brother looked torn, but in the end he shrugged. "Okay," he said, then stood up and held out his hand to Gunner. "Thank you."

Gunner shook it. "Anything I can do to help make this better for the people Willa loves gives me purpose."

Chance glanced at me and smirked. "You got a good one."

"I know," I replied. Gunner was one of the things I believed God had given me to make up for the mother I'd been born to. I wanted Chance to find the same thing in life.

CHAPTER SIX

WILLA

When I had woken up this morning, Gunner was gone and a note was lying on his pillow. I had rubbed my eyes, then sat up and taken the note to read:

Meet me at the tree house

Confused, since the tree house was not on Nonna's property but on the former Lawton estate's property, I had decided to go with it. Maybe he was moving it today so that Bella could use it when she visited Nonna. Deciding that was most likely what was happening, I hurried to get dressed, then grabbed one of the brownies Nonna had sent over on my way out of the house. No one else seemed to be at home, or they were still in bed.

Deciding not to park at the former Lawton estate since the new owners may call the cops if a strange car was in their driveway, I parked at Nonna's and took my old path to the tree house. It had been over six years since I'd taken this walk. That had been the day that Gunner first told me he loved me. Smiling at the memory, I headed down to figure out what he was up to.

Maybe he had wanted me to bring Bella . . . but then he hadn't mentioned it. The note had been simple and exactly like the one he had left for me six years ago. As I came through the woods into the clearing, I saw him leaning against the tree with his arms crossed over his chest, waiting for me. His eyes met mine, and he smiled.

"We're trespassing, you know," I told him as I reached him.

He shrugged. "I've never followed rules. You know that."

I laughed. "I'm hoping the owners know what we are doing."

He nodded slowly. "They do. They're very aware of what we are doing."

I raised my eyebrows. "Okay, that's good. Are you going to tell me what we are doing?" I glanced up at the tree house. It was neglected and in need of repair. I hoped we weren't going up there, because I wasn't sure we would be safe.

"It needs some work," he said to me, noticing where my gaze had gone.

"Are you moving it to Nonna's property for Bella?" I asked him. Knowing that my sister was going to be a part of our life now made the ache inside me from all I had missed ease. The idea of making something for her permanent at Nonna's felt good.

"If you want to move it we can," he replied with a secretive gleam in his eyes.

"Definitely. I thought that was what . . ." But whatever words I was about to say stalled on my lips as Gunner Lawton walked to stand in front of me, then sank down on one knee.

Of all the things I could have imagined would happen this morning, this was not one of them. My world had been a roller coaster of emotions since I had sat down at Nonna's for pie yesterday morning. Today I had planned on spending more time with Chance and Bella while Gunner went to the field to help Ryker and Nash do some things. Never had I thought we would be here in this moment.

"I fell in love with you in this spot, twice. I felt like it was the only place worthy of this question," he said as he opened the ring box and the most beautiful oval sapphire outlined in tiny diamonds glistened in the sunlight. "It's been forever for us since the beginning. We both knew it. I've waited until the right time, and that time always seems wrong. It's never special enough. But yesterday our life changed. For the better. You've been given a chance to have your family back. I want us to be a part of that. The time is right now. I'm ready to make our forever official. Willa, will you marry me?"

I reached down and touched the ring in his hand, then lifted my gaze from it to look at him. As wild as this sounded in the middle of all that was happening, I knew that this moment was right no matter when and where it happened. With all the changes that were coming to my life I wanted this one to be a part of it. "Yes. You know it's a yes," I said softly.

He smirked and shrugged one shoulder. "Let's just say I didn't have any doubts."

Laughing at him, I took his hand and pulled him back up so I could properly kiss him. He held up his hand to hold me off. "Wait," he said. "Patience." He then took my left hand and slid the beautiful ring onto my finger. "Now, have your way with me," he said as his hands took my waist and pulled me against him.

I kissed him, holding his face in my hands. I'd known

one day we would take this step, and now that we had, my chest felt so full I was sure it would combust with happiness. The despair that had filled me yesterday had slowly began to fade after last night at Nonna's. This morning, Gunner had managed to take it all away. To give me even more of a reason to have hope for tomorrow and all that was to come.

"I love you, Gunner Lawton," I said against his lips.

"And that makes me the luckiest bastard on the planet," he said, pulling back from me and breaking the kiss. I wasn't done yet. I was even considering testing the tree house out.

"We have time for that later. Lots of time. But first I thought you'd like to look around our house, just for a refresher, so that you can start buying furniture," he told me as he took my hand and started walking farther away from Nonna's. "We have plenty of bedrooms, so if you want to bring Bella by later today, she could pick out one she wants. You can decorate it with her, then she can come visit anytime she wants. Maybe spend summers with us. Chance will need a break."

I didn't move. "What house?" I asked as the realization started dawning on me. The possibility of what he meant sinking in.

He grinned at me. "You miss it here, don't you? You miss your nonna. Being close to her," he said.

I nodded. "Yes, but with you is where I belong. Wherever you are."

He growled and pulled me against him. "Keep talking like that and I'm going to take your sexy ass right up against that tree." Then he pressed a quick kiss to my lips. "It's a good thing, then, that you'll get all you want. Because I bought back the Lawton estate. This will be our home in a few weeks. Give Bella a bedroom. Hell, give Chance a fucking bedroom if it makes you happy."

"Are you serious?" I asked him, my jaw falling open. Unable to believe this was happening. I hadn't even realized he wanted to come back here. I thought that he hated it here. I wouldn't even bring it up. But now . . . he'd . . . done this.

"Yes, baby. This is all yours. We're home. Lawton is where we belong."

RYKER AND AURORA

"The days of our youth were behind us."

CHAPTER ONE

RYKER

A hand gripped my shoulder with a hard squeeze. I turned my head to look at my dad.

"It's done," I told him, then turned my gaze back to the football facility that had once been an open field where parties were held.

"I'm proud of you and Nash. This is really something," he said. "Not that being in the NFL isn't impressive. I'm damn proud of that, but this is more. It's doing something with what you've accomplished in life."

Even with the buildings, lights, and parking lot, I could still see how it once was. A big open field with a bonfire, trucks, a keg, and my friends. It was a memory I'd feared I would never get back after the night Hunter was killed here. Time heals. Hunter's death would always be something that changed me. It changed us all, but I could remember the good times here too.

"Hunter would love this," I said.

"Yeah, he would be fucking proud," Dad replied. "I like to think he'll be here on Saturday. Listening to his sister stand in front of all those people and talk about him and what this place will do for so many kids."

I nodded, feeling my chest fill with pride at the fact that Aurora was going to speak. She had gotten more secure with her voice over the past few years, but this was a big deal. I'd have never asked her to do it. She'd asked to, and I had fought back tears, I'd been so damn proud of her. My girl was the bravest person in the world.

"When are you going to put a ring on it, son?" Dad asked.

I turned to look back at him. "After this. I wanted this dedication to her brother to be the focus. It means as much to her family as it does to us. But when it's all done and we are back in Texas, I've got it all ready and set up."

Dad grinned. "'Ready and set up'? What are you going to do?"

"I'm a Dallas Cowboy. I have some power and connections," I replied with a smirk.

He laughed then. "Not at all cocky about it either."

"Some things don't change," I said.

He shook his head, still smiling. "No, they don't."

"I'm going to put in a full five years in the NFL, then we are moving home, but I don't want to wait until then to get married. I've been ready for that since the moment I met her."

Dad nodded. "You fell hard and fast. Pretty little red-head with her freckles and curls wrapped you up quick. That's for damn sure."

"When you find the one, you know. Even if it's in high school," I replied.

"I guess so. Seems most of you boys did."

I thought about Nash and Tallulah. It was so fucking nice to see him happy again. When he had broken it off with her he'd been a different person. When he had hurt his leg and his football career ended, I'd thought that would be the darkest I ever saw him. But I had been wrong. Losing Tallulah had destroyed him.

"I reckon I need to head back to the house. Your momma is cooking some casseroles for me to take to the Maclays. With all the company they got coming into town and staying with them for Saturday, she's trying to help feed them."

I nodded. "I'll be back shortly and can take the food over there."

"All righty," he replied before walking back toward the parking lot.

I made my way down to the main offices to lock up and grab the helmet order that had to be filled out by tomorrow. Nash was handling all that, and I wasn't sure where he was with the count.

Making millions of dollars for playing football was something I'd always talked about as a kid. Now that I was doing it, having something like this to invest it into made what I'd accomplished mean something. The game had always come so easily to me. But this had taken hard work and would continue to require more from me. It was something far bigger than an NFL career.

CHAPTER TWO

AURORA

Nahla had offered to drive me to my dad's. I realized my hand was gripping the door handle tightly and tried to relax. It wasn't that far of a drive, and Nahla had passed her driver's test, although that had just been two months ago.

I could hear her laughing when she noticed me hanging on to the door, and I moved my hand back to my lap and smiled at her. "Sorry," I said.

She shrugged. "It's fine. My mom does the same thing, and she gasps a lot too. At least you do it quietly."

Ryker's younger sister had become a beauty. She turned heads everywhere she went. Nahla was the head cheerleader, prom queen, and head of the student government at Lawton High School. She was dating a football player, but he hadn't come around after the first day we were here. Ryker had threatened him if he ever hurt Nahla. Nahla had been humiliated and furious, but the poor boy had gone white as a ghost.

Their mother said it was a good thing Ryker didn't live here during Nahla's high school years. I had to agree with that. He was not handling the fact his sister wasn't a little girl anymore well. In his eyes, Nahla should still be in pigtails, playing with dolls.

When Nahla's car pulled into my dad's driveway, I sighed in relief as quietly as I could. I hadn't lived here since December of what would have been my senior year. I had taken summer school so that I could graduate early. After Christmas, I had my high school diploma, and Ryker had come home for the holidays.

He had moved me to Oklahoma with him, although my dad had been upset about it. Ryker had convinced me he couldn't stay away from me any longer, and I felt the same. So I went and graduated from the University of Oklahoma. Ryker was drafted to the Cowboys in the first round last year, and we moved to Texas, which was where we were now.

I missed Lawton, but I wanted to be where Ryker was. Visiting here was enough. I made it back to North Carolina to see Gran more than I made it here. Whenever Ryker had to be in California for a game or event, I made sure to visit my mom. Hunter would have wanted me to come back and see Dad, but I did it because I wanted to. After Hunter's death, I grew much closer to my dad. We had needed each other during that time. Hunter had meant the world to both of us, and we understood the other's grief.

"I'm going over to Van's, but I'll stop by later to see everyone," Nahla told me.

"Okay," I replied. I had known she was headed to her boyfriend's when she'd come out of her room dressed to impress. "Be careful," I added, suddenly feeling like a parent.

She grinned and nodded. Before I made it to the front door, her car was out of the driveway and headed down the street. If Ryker ever caught her driving that fast, he'd freak out. Turning, I went to the door, knocked once, then stepped inside.

The smell of Gran's cobbler met my nose, and I smiled. She was here! Dropping my purse on the side table, I hurried to the kitchen. It had been over two months since I had visited her in North Carolina. She turned when she heard my footsteps, and her big wide smile that crinkled her cheeks and made her eyes twinkle warmed me up inside.

"Gran!" I said, then rushed into her open arms.

"There's my beautiful girl. I've made blueberry cobbler with blueberries I brought with me straight from Mo Taylor's field. Nice and fresh Carolina blueberries," she told me. "I was hoping you'd get here while it was still warm."

There was a time my grandmother didn't care much for my father, and she wouldn't ever have considered staying at his house or cooking in his kitchen, but death changes things. Hunter's changed so much in my family. My parents got along now. My stepmother and mom even talked on the phone often. Hunter would have loved to see this.

"Do we have vanilla ice cream?" I asked her hopefully.

"We didn't, but we do now. I sent your daddy to the store once I got here. And Ryker's momma called to say she'd made us some casseroles and was bringing them over. That's a good family." She patted my arm. "Good man you got too."

"Yes, they are," I agreed.

"Now sit. Let me feed you. It's good for my soul," she told me as she motioned toward the table. "Denver wanted me to tell you he was sorry they couldn't make it. Sandy is due to have that baby any day now, you know."

I nodded. "Yeah, I saw that on Facebook. I sent them tiny Dallas Cowboys jersey as a baby gift," I told her. Denver, my first boyfriend and longest friend, had gotten married two years ago to a girl from the school I used to attend with them in North Carolina.

Gran laughed. "Sending a Panthers fan a Cowboys jersey. That's a good one."

I smiled at her and shrugged. "I told him that he could wear it when I come to visit. I also sent them the high chair they were registered for, if that makes it better."

Gran placed a slice of cobbler with a scoop of vanilla ice cream on top in front of me. "Eat. You're always too thin. You need to eat more," she scolded. It was something she'd been fussing about for as long as I could remember.

I didn't need to be told twice. I had just put the first bite in my mouth when my dad came walking into the kitchen. "That smells too good for me to stay in my office," he said, then he looked at me. "Hello, honey. I see you didn't waste time getting some."

"Girl needs to eat. Now you sit and I'll get you a slice," Gran told him.

He winked at me and thanked Gran before taking the chair across the table from me. "Where's Ryker?"

"Still at the field. He's bringing over casseroles his momma made later."

"I have a few things I want him to sign. I've got some business associates who are Cowboys fans," he said.

This was nothing new. Dad had Ryker sign things most every visit. Hunter would think that was hilarious. I smiled, imagining him being here watching us now. I often felt like he was. It was a peaceful feeling that would come over me. When I was alone and it happened, I would talk to him as if he were there.

"Okay," I replied, then took another bite.

"You still up for the dedication? Talking, that is?" he asked, a concerned frown between his brows.

"Yes. I'm nervous, sure, but I need to do this. Hunter would want me to," I told him. I always believed Hunter would be there. We might not be able to see him, but he wouldn't miss this. I was going to make him proud.

"Good girl," Dad said as he reached over and squeezed my hand.

CHAPTER THREE

RYKER

When Aurora's expression changed from one of enjoyment to tension, I knew it was time for us to leave. So much talking and visiting was wearing on her. I made our excuses and got her to the silence of the SUV.

"Thanks," she said softly.

I leaned over and kissed her. "You're welcome, but it was a little selfish on my part. I wanted you to myself."

She laughed and kissed me once more before leaning back in her seat with a sigh. "They can get loud, can't they?" she said.

"Oh yeah, but so can my bunch," I replied.

We drove in silence, and I knew she needed it. After

living most of her life in her own world of silence, being overstimulated with noise could wear her down. Going back to my parents' wasn't going to be any better. My aunt and uncle were there, and I knew they'd all be drinking and eating the ridiculous amounts of food my momma had made today.

Instead I drove us to the back side of the Lee property, which had remained untouched. I hadn't been back there in years, but there was a pond, and it would be a good spot to look up at the sky. When we drove past my parents' house, she looked over at me but didn't ask.

There were no clouds tonight, and it was unusually cool for May in the south. There was no chance of her getting cold, but she wouldn't get hot, either. These were the rare nights that Alabama got in the spring that should be enjoyed.

When I parked the truck, I glanced over at her. "It's quieter here. My house would have been just as noisy."

"That sounds nice," she said, then reached to open her door and climb out. I hurried around to make sure she didn't trip over any branches, then let down the tailgate and picked her up to place her in the back of my father's new Ford. She scooted back, and I climbed in beside her.

"It's a clear night, and we can look at the stars. Only talk when you want to," I told her.

She smiled so sweetly up at me, I felt that familiar possessive tug in my gut that only Aurora could do to me. The moonlight made her green eyes, which I'd been obsessed with since the moment I saw her in the entryway of Lawton High School, sparkle.

"You keep looking at me like that and I won't be able to do more than gaze at your eyes. Those fucking stars don't even compare."

She laughed softly, then leaned over to lay her head on my chest. "You and your thing with my eyes," she whispered.

"If our kids don't all get your eyes, I'm going to need a refund," I teased.

She laughed harder this time, then tilted her head back to look at me. "What if I want them to have your eyes?"

I sighed dramatically just to make her laugh more. "Fine. One can have my eyes, but that's all I will accept."

Aurora lifted her hand to touch my cheek. "Exactly how many kids are we going to have?"

I shrugged. "Depends. I want a girl with auburn curls and green eyes. We will have to keep trying until I get one."

She grinned, then pressed her lips against mine in a chaste kiss. "I love you," she whispered.

"And that makes me the luckiest damn man on the planet," I said.

She eased back down and moved her hand to my chest. "You mean that, don't you?" she asked.

"You shouldn't have to ask me that. You should know it."

Aurora tilted her head to the side, and her curls fell over her shoulder. Nothing was more beautiful than this woman. "But you have women, sexy, gorgeous women, throw themselves at you. I've seen them try. I know when I can't be at a game that it happens probably more so."

I didn't like this conversation. I shifted my body toward her and took her face in my hands so I had her complete attention. Sure, most of my teammates had a different girl in their beds every weekend. If I was being honest, they had several different girls in their beds every weekend. But I wasn't like them. I wasn't searching for something to fill that part of me.

"There is no one more beautiful than you. Everything about you since the moment I saw you has drawn me in. It took one week with you to change me for life. They can't do that. They are just faces. I see nothing there. No pull. All I know is when I step off that field you are waiting on me, and I can't fucking wait to be with you." I stopped talking and took her hand, then placed it over my heart. "This is yours. Always will be."

She beamed up at me. "I know. It just amazes me. Seeing your boyfriend on magazine covers, on television, having people stop him to ask if he is Ryker Lee . . . it can be intimidating. I love it, don't get me wrong. You are living your dream, and I love that. You did it. I am so proud of you. I just have my moments when I wonder if I am enough."

This was not what I wanted to hear, but if she's thinking this, I was damn glad she'd told me. I needed to clear this shit up now. I moved and leaned against the truck, then pulled her into my lap, facing me. "You wonder if you're enough? Aurora, I'm the only one who should have that fear. You are the bravest person I know. You're kind, giving, you make differences in the world, and you're breathtakingly beautiful. I can catch a ball and run fast. I've not overcome anything. And I'm not as fucking gorgeous as you are. So, baby, it is me that should be intimidated," I told her. "I see men looking at you. Everywhere we go. I'm just thankful I'm big enough that it scares them the fuck off," I added, and she giggled.

"You are crazy, Ryker Lee."

I cupped her face in my hands. "Hell yeah, I am. I've been crazy about you from day one. That will never change."

"I'm pretty crazy about you too," she said softly.

I wish we had blankets in the back of this damn truck. I tried to think of some way to make it more comfortable, but I had no supplies. I leaned forward and kissed the tip of her nose.

"We have two options, because I'm now hard as a rock and I need to be reaffirmed," I told her. "We can climb back in the truck and act like we are teens or go back to my parents', sneak in the back, and go straight to my room."

She made a small gasping noise when she wiggled enough in my lap to see I was being honest about my situation. "What's wrong with right here?" she asked.

"There's no cushions or blankets," I said, getting more worked up at the thought of it.

"We don't need them. I think I've proven I'm not breakable already," she said in a saucy tone, then sat back and began to pull her shirt up over her head.

The back of the truck it was, then.

CHAPTER FOUR

AURORA

Tallulah was my first friend in Lawton. The day I was faced with going to a regular high school instead of the school for the hearing impaired I had always attended, I'd been so nervous. She had made it easier. Her ability to use sign language, after taking a summer class on it one year, had instantly eased me, and I hadn't felt like I had to rely on Hunter for everything.

She had called me, devastated, after Nash and her had broken up, and I'd flown to Chicago to spend time with her. Having them back together made everything perfect for the dedication. Nash and Ryker were cousins, but they acted like brothers. Their families were very close, and

I liked to think one day Tallulah and I would be family. I couldn't imagine Nash with anyone else. He'd been unable to move on after they'd broken up. It had worried Ryker. We'd spent many nights talking about it.

The day that Nash had bought a new truck, he had gotten drunk and called Ryker. His drunken ramblings had said that he couldn't get in his old truck. That Tallulah was all over it. He had found one of her hair ties that day and lost it. Gone and traded it in, then gone home to get drunk because his new truck didn't smell like her.

She wasn't one to share much except when she was hurting, but reading people's expressions was something I was good at. I knew that as much fun as we were having this morning, drinking mimosas while watching Riley, Willa, and Maggie try on wedding dresses, Tallulah was envious.

Part of me understood that, but something in Tallulah's eyes was different. Almost as if she feared she wasn't going to get this. This had been a last-minute trip put together by Willa. She had pointed out it could be hard to get us all together again and she wanted us all there when she picked out her dress, and Riley and Maggie agreed.

"Not that one," Maggie said when Riley walked out in the newest dress she had tried on. "The one before was way better. You have great boobs. That one doesn't show them off."

Riley laughed. "Noted," she replied. "When are you going to try on the second one you picked out?" she asked Maggie.

"In a minute," she said, then held up her drink to take a sip.

"That's just juice. The champagne is over there," Willa told her, pointing at the table across from me.

It was just a moment, a second really, that her expression faltered. I thought perhaps it was just me who'd seen it, but Willa had seen it too. She gasped loudly. "OH MY GOD!" she squealed, then clapped her hands together.

Maggie's face turned slightly red, then she looked at me as if she were apologizing. "I'm sorry. This weekend is about the field. About Hunter's memory and legacy. With all the other things that have happened, I just didn't want to add to it. This isn't about me." She said the words so quickly, if I didn't have the implant I wouldn't have understood her. I couldn't have read her lips that fast.

"What?" Riley asked, looking from Maggie to me then at Willa.

"Everything that has happened since we all got back to town has been perfect. Hunter would have wanted all this happiness."

"What am I missing? Did someone else get engaged?" Riley asked, looking from me to Ezmita to Tallulah.

"I'm pregnant." Maggie said the words, then burst into a huge smile as tears welled up in her eyes.

Willa wrapped her arms around her and started squealing again.

"It's about time one of you got knocked up," Riley said, beaming, then went to hug Maggie too.

I glanced at Tallulah and saw it there again. A fear or sadness. I wanted to talk to her about it, but I didn't know where or how to even begin. There were moments when I wondered if Ryker was going to ask me to marry him but we had time. I knew he loved me and that or future was together. I wasn't hurting by watching this all take place. I was happy for them. All of them.

The congratulations continued, and tears were shed. I drank another mimosa and tried to follow all the chatter, but it could be difficult. Seeing Maggie so happy was what mattered. When the brides all went back to try on more dresses, Tallulah let out a sigh and a small laugh, then stood up. "I need a refill."

"Me too," Ezmita said, standing up to follow Tallulah.

"Life is happening fast. We all got together, and it went on hyperspeed," I said.

Tallulah handed Ezmita a glass, then took hers to sit back down. "No kidding," she said, then leaned back on the white leather sofa. "I didn't expect so much change when we got here. I had hoped I could make it through seeing Nash. I never expected all the engagements, moves, and now a baby."

"I'm going to miss this," I said. "When we left, I forgot how great this was to be with all of you. To have my friends."

Tallulah's smile held no sadness this time as she reached over and squeezed my hand. "We have three weddings and a baby coming up. We will be getting together several times in the next year."

She was right. There would be many reasons for us to all be in the same place very soon. "I hadn't thought of that."

"Tomorrow is the dedication. When is everyone leaving?" Ezmita asked.

"We have to leave Sunday morning early," I told her.

"I have to go back to Chicago and pack up, close out the lease on my apartment, but then I'll be back," Tallulah told her.

"I think Maggie and West are leaving Sunday too. Willa and Gunner are here to stay," I said.

"What about this one?" Maggie asked, and we all turned to look at her. It dawned on me then that her wedding would either have to be soon or more than nine months from now.

"It's stunning," I said. "But have y'all set a date for the wedding? That may impact the dress choice."

"True, you have a growing stomach to think about," Tallulah added.

Maggie grinned. "Next month."

"What?!" Willa asked, turning to her. "How are you going to do that?"

Maggie placed a hand on her stomach. "I want to before the baby comes and before I have a big round stomach, making it hard to find a dress. So we are doing simple. Right here in Lawton. I just don't know where yet."

This was all happening. It was real. Our lives were moving on to the next step. The days of our youth were behind us. It was such an odd yet exciting feeling. I assumed Brady and Riley would be next. They had been engaged almost a year. Riley had said that so much had been happening this past year they had wanted to wait until things settled down.

My thoughts went to my future with Ryker. Where would we be in a year, two years? Would we be married? Would we all be able to get together so I could try on dresses? Or would that take place in Texas? I glanced over at Tallulah again to see her smiling happily and realized what she must have been thinking about. Because I was wondering the same things now. When would our lives begin this next journey?

CHAPTER FIVE

RYKER

The firepit that we had brought over from Nash's house was safely roaring with a fire in the middle of the back field, which sat directly where the field parties were once held. Tomorrow the dedication would happen on the front field, but tonight our own sort of dedication would take place.

The last field party.

Damn, that felt weird to say. We hadn't partied out here in five years, but knowing this was the last one was hard to accept. Even though our lives were so different now. I wasn't that cocky asshole standing in the bed of his truck like he owned the world. I wasn't full of foolish pride.

"Should I get chairs?" Nash called out from the field house.

"Fuck no! We aren't that damn old yet," I told him.

"We need some old tires and stumps," West said as he tapped the keg that we'd brought out here.

"I have blankets in the car. I forgot to get them," Riley added.

"Be right back," Brady replied, understanding that was his cue to go get them.

"Who needs blankets? It's grass," West asked, looking insulted.

"I do—you know, the pregnant one," Maggie told him.

None of us pretended our women hadn't already told us. There was no point. They knew we'd been told already.

"Congratulations, by the way," I said to them both.

West grinned and pulled Maggie up against his side and kissed the top of her head. "Thanks," he replied, looking real damn pleased with himself.

"I brought a veggie tray," Willa said, walking toward us. "I sent Gunner back to the Rover for the ranch dip."

"Oh, thank God!" Maggie said, looking thrilled.

"Gunner let you bring a veggie tray to a field party?" I asked, slightly horrified.

Willa raised her eyebrows. "Gunner doesn't tell me what to do," she said.

"Jesus, woman. You're killing my reputation," Gunner said as he caught up to her.

"Wine, Gunner? Seriously?" I asked, seeing the bottle of red wine in his other hand.

He shrugged then nodded at Willa. "It's her fault."

"Looks like there's more food," Nash said, grinning, and nodded his head toward Asa and Ezmita, who had just walked through the gate. There was a large bag that I recognized from the Stop and Shop.

"Please, God, let that be cinnamon rolls," I said.

"Oh, so those are okay? Just not veggies?" Willa asked me.

"It's cinnamon rolls, baby. You gotta understand," Gunner told her, causing her to roll her eyes.

Brady was back, putting out the blankets, when Tallulah arrived with several bakery boxes and a bottle of sparkling apple cider. By the time it was all set up, the last field party looked more like someone was having a reception. Although we were using red Solo cups, there was champagne, red wine, sparkling apple cider for Maggie, and paper plates instead of just the keg of beer. Tallulah had even produced a roll of paper towels from Nash's office. The night had fallen, and the fire was blazing. We had our friends, and we were all together.

"To the field that raised us," Nash said, raising his red Solo cup into the air.

"To the field!" everyone said together before taking a drink.

"When did we get so damn fancy? Domestic and shit?" Gunner asked, taking another drink of his beer, then reaching for a cinnamon roll.

"Would you have preferred some bags of chips like the old days?" Willa asked him, smirking.

He shrugged, then grunted. "We rarely had chips then. Just the keg."

"Fuck no," West said as he chomped down on one of Tallulah's mom's brownies. "This is way better."

"It's the last field party. It should be special. Stand out," Asa said, sitting with his arm around Ezmita, who I realized had never come to a field party. She was leaning back on his chest, and it was clear he was happy. Out of all of us, he had made the biggest transformation.

"I don't think it could stand out any more than it already does. Three couples engaged, one having a baby, folks moving back to Lawton and settling down," I said. Aurora was snuggled up to my side with wine in her cup. She hadn't experienced many field parties herself.

"And we got a fucking football celebrity in our midst," West said. "Who knew one of us would go big," he added.

Then the other guys all said together, "I did."

I laughed and looked at Nash.

"What?" he said. "We all knew you would be the one to make it. You were our star. Everyone knew that."

I shrugged. I had wanted it, but I hadn't been as sure as they had. Back then my world had been rocked by the woman at my side. She had given me more to want in life than football. I wasn't so sure I could have done any of this had she not been there with me. When I needed her she always had the right words. She was my biggest fan and the center of my world.

"I'm not a celebrity," I finally said.

Gunner laughed. "Dude, there are paintings and photographs of you doing incredible plays at Oklahoma for sale all over the internet. Google it."

I reached for another cookie, wishing they'd talk about someone or something else. At home, with Aurora, I was just me. It was the two of us. She made my world complete. If I was injured tomorrow and had to end my career I would be fine. Just as long as I had her with me. One day soon I wanted a ring on my hand telling everyone I belong to her. I want to see her stomach grow with our child and to see her hold our baby. I was ready for all of that. It was what mattered. Not my career. Not football.

"I need to know how much you had to pay to get your house back, Gunner," Nash said, taking the attention off me. He knew I didn't like it.

Gunner shrugged. "Enough."

Asa laughed along with West.

"He paid a fucking fortune," Brady said. "That's what 'enough' means in Gunner talk."

Eventually the conversation fell into everyone's plans, wedding dates, and where they would have them. I smiled, thinking about the fact that they'd have another wedding to put on their calendars soon enough. I didn't expect it to surprise them, just as I knew Nash was making his own plans to put a ring on Tallulah.

I figured Asa and Ezmita would be the last of us to walk down the aisle. They were the newest couple. But I had no doubt they would end up there. Asa had never really gotten over her to begin with. We all knew it.

"In ten years, let's come back. Make it a tradition. Leave the kids at home, bring the damn food, and come back for this. Our new grown-up-style field party, as disgusting, yet filling and delicious, as it may be," West said.

I had no doubt in ten years we would all be here. The boys of Lawton High had found their forever. That wasn't going to change. Even if our lives continued to.

CHAPTER SIX

RYKER

Nash stood beside me just inside the entrance of the gates to Hunter Maclay Field. Cars would start to arrive soon. The dedication was to begin in an hour. Aurora was getting ready with Tallulah in the offices. She was nervous and Tallulah had promised me that she would help reassure her as well as convince her to have a glass of the champagne that was chilling in the boardroom. When this was finished, our families would go inside to a reception. We would all need a drink by then.

"This is it," he said. "What we have worked for."

I slapped him on the back. "I didn't do much. Not compared to you. This is your idea. You drew out the plans, you pitched it, you built this."

He smirked as he looked over at me. "None of which I could have done without your money and the investors you got involved."

I shrugged. "My part was easier. What you've done here is something I will forever be grateful to you for. I may even let you beat me at a game of pool."

He chuckled. "I doubt it."

"Yeah, you're probably right," I agreed.

We were silent a moment as the first car pulled into the parking lot. It was Aurora's dad. "What you did for them, for Aurora, for Hunter . . . it really is fucking incredible," I told him.

Nash shrugged. "I wanted to have something like this. To build it and give kids a future, or at least some hope. Hunter was one of us. He didn't get to fall in love . . . or come to the last field party. I couldn't think of a better name for the place. Besides, you're the one who is funding the scholarship in his name."

"He would have been my brother-in-law one day," I said. "And that wasn't the last field party. Remember in ten years we're having another one."

He chuckled. "I'd like to think we will, but who knows where we will all be, what we will be doing."

I wanted to argue, but he was right. We didn't know what the future held for all of us.

"Last night was good," I told him. "We all needed it."

"Yeah, it was. Even with the spread of food and girly drinks," he replied.

More cars began to pull into the parking lot, and we waited to greet them all as they walked through the gates.

With the stands packed full of family, friends, and people from this town we had known all our lives I watched as Aurora stepped forward to the microphone. I was so fucking nervous because I wanted to be up there holding her hand. I knew this was a big deal for her, and I was struggling to let her do it without me.

"Thank you for being here today," she began. That smile that owned me lit up her face, and I watched as she glanced at the notes she had written, then put them down as if she had decided not to use them.

"I entered this world with a best friend. Not everyone is blessed with that, but I was. We shared our mother's womb, a baby bed, a bedroom, a trampoline, and a swing set. With my brother, I was always accepted. He never treated me differently like other kids would do when they realized I spoke with my hands. When I was with him, it was as if nothing were different about me at all. He was my twin brother, my very first friend, my protector, even when I wished he would back off a bit."

Laughter spread across the crowd, and I felt a lump so damn big in my throat that I wasn't sure I could swallow.

"Hunter Maclay will always be a part of me. There are times I swear he is right beside me. I feel a peace, and I know it's him. And today, as I look out over all of you and this facility, I am . . ." She paused and took a deep breath. I could see the struggle in her features. My own eyes were fighting back tears. "I am honored that he will be remembered this way. With such an amazing place. He would love to know kids were given this opportunity to play the sport I believe he was born loving."

I wiped at my eyes before the tears could fall. Aurora continued to talk about the work put into the place. She thanked the investors, and she thanked my family for the donation of the land. I wasn't sure there was a dry eye in the stands when she stepped back and Nash whispered to her and hugged her before taking the microphone.

I waited until she moved behind the stage to walk across the grass and go to her. She had not only spoken in front of hundreds of people, she had used her voice. With all her fear that her voice was different, she had overcome that. My long strides got me to her quickly, and when she turned to me I pulled her into my arms.

"You were incredible," I said into her hair.

"I sounded okay?" she asked me.

"Baby, your voice is the sweetest damn sound on the earth. I've told you that a million times."

"But you love me," she replied.

I looked down at her. "Oh, it's more than love. *Worship*, *adore*, those are closer descriptions."

She laughed softly. "I worship and adore you too."

"Good, because I'm keeping you."

She nodded. "You better."

I tucked a strand of her hair behind her ear. "You didn't even look nervous."

The soft smile that spread across her lips made me want to kiss her for hours.

"I wasn't alone," she said. "Hunter was there. I could feel him. It was as if he were so close he was holding my hand. As if I could have reached out and touched him. It may sound silly, but it was real. He was with me up there."

I shook my head. "That doesn't sound silly. I don't think he would have missed this for anything."

Her eyes glistened with tears. "Me either. Just like when we were kids, he showed up to keep me from having to do something alone. He was always like that. I shouldn't have expected him to be a no-show today."

I pulled her to my chest and held her. "He'll always show up for the important stuff, baby."

And he would. I knew he would. That was Hunter Maclay.

ONE MONTH LATER

"The game may be finished, but now we have the future."

WEST

I stood looking out over Lawton. In the exact spot my dad and I used to stand and the same place I had brought Maggie. This was the perfect location. When Maggie had suggested it when we were trying to decide on the location of our wedding, I had been surprised. Sure, it had a good view, but it wasn't a church. It didn't have flower gardens or anything flashy that most women want.

Although the transformation the girls had pulled off had made it pretty damn magical. I had known this day would come, and I think my dad had too. He'd loved Maggie on sight, but then she was hard not to love. I sure as hell had tried not to love her. Stupid punk kid I'd been hadn't deserved her. I was thankful she'd seen through all my anger and pain to find someone worth saving.

"You ready to do this?" Brady asked as he came to stand beside me.

"You know that answer," I replied.

He sighed. "Yeah, I reckon I do. Guess it seems right you two are the first to walk down the aisle and have a baby. You were the first of us to fall hard."

I smirked. "You weren't that far behind me."

"I won't be in the marrying step either. I'm more than ready for Riley and Bryony to be Higgens. I know they're mine, but I want that last step."

"I understand that," I replied.

We stood there looking out over the town that had raised us. Through all the good times, wins, losses, heart-break, and our darkest moments, we had known that was home. We had that one secure thing to hold on to. Not everyone had that, and I knew we were damn lucky. It was more than just football pads, helmets, fresh-cut grass, the smell of the cowhide. It was a friendship that made us a family. We would always have that, even if our days playing on a field together were over. It had taught us a lot about life, prepared us for things to come—and we had thought we were just playing a sport we loved.

"We were lucky," I said, breaking the silence.

Brady turned to look at me, but I continued to take in the view.

"To have had this. One another," I finished.

"Yeah, we were . . . we are. The game may be finished, but now we have the future."

I smiled. "That's what I was thinking."

"West." A familiar voice said my name, and I turned to see my mother standing there. I hadn't expected her to be here. I knew this was Maggie's doing. She'd wanted me to talk to my mom, but I hadn't been able to do it. Not after she had gotten married and hadn't thought to tell me until after.

"Hello, Mother," I replied.

Brady slapped my back, then walked away, leaving us there. Part of me wished he'd have stayed to be a buffer or distraction.

She looked nervous as she twisted her hands together. I was good at reading her body language. Once we had been close. Once she had been a mother to me. That had died with my dad. She told me what I had already figured out. "Maggie told me about the wedding."

I nodded. "Sounds like Maggie."

She bit her lip, and I could see the unshed tears glistening in her eyes. I didn't want to see my momma cry. God knows I'd seen enough of that in my past, but I also couldn't just forgive her and act like the past six years hadn't happened.

"She's a beautiful bride, but I knew she would be," Mom said.

I knew Maggie would be stunning. That wasn't what Mom wanted to talk about, and today wasn't the day I wanted to have a heart-to-heart with her. This was the day I married the woman I would spend my life with. The woman who had not once let me down or turned her back on me. When I needed someone the most, she was there. I couldn't say the same for my mother.

"She invited you, and you came. It's good to see you again. Thanks for coming," I said, then started to walk away.

"West, please. I need to say something. I need to explain."

"No, you don't. Not here and not today. The time for that has passed."

"Honey, please," she pleaded, and her voice broke. The lone tear rolling down her cheek made me think of Dad. He never wanted Mom to cry. He loved her laugh. I was making her cry, and although she didn't deserve this, I couldn't do it.

"Okay, fine. I'm listening. Just stop crying."

She sniffled and wiped away her tear and the next one about to fall. "I am sorry. That's something I haven't said and I should. I am truly sorry. I lost myself when we lost your dad. I should have been there for you. I should have been a mother, but I was struggling to make it. You left for college, and the little bit of progress I had made at being a mom again was lost. I was lonely and sad. I didn't think I'd ever be happy again. I searched for it. Seeing you reminded me of all we had and lost. I felt guilty when I looked at you, and I knew how disappointed your father would be with me.

"I ran from that life. Our life. Lawton. All of it. And I hurt you. I'm so sorry . . . and I know you aren't okay with me being married. It's why I waited to tell you. I was afraid of how you would take it. But I'm happy again. I don't feel lost anymore. And I know I can't erase the past, but I want to change how things are now. I want to be a mom to you . . . and a grandmother." The sadness, hope, and fear in her eyes made it difficult to lash out. I didn't understand my mother. I doubted I ever would, but she was my mom. I had never stopped loving her or needing her in my life. I had just learned to live without her.

"You're right. I don't understand. I never will, but I forgive you. It was never me keeping you out of my life. That has been your decision. If you want to be a mother and a grandmother, then do it. Show me. The ball is in your court here," I told her.

She gave me a teary smile. "Really?"

"It always has been, Mom," I replied.

She stepped closer to me, and I knew what she wanted. I opened my arms and she walked into them as I held her. She sniffled against my chest, and I looked out over the town.

It's going to be okay, Dad, I mouthed, because I had no doubt he was there watching.

GUNNER

Wearing a tux sucked. I hated dressing up, but this year would be full of this. Weddings out the ass. I grinned, thinking about the fact one of those would be mine. Standing at the edge of the setup, I saw West talking to his mother. There was so much damage in that shit. It looked like they were having a long-past-due talk. His dad's death had messed that family up. He'd always had the life I wanted growing up, until it all fell apart.

Not that my shitty family had been better. There would be no making up with my mom on my wedding day. She wasn't interested in that, and there had been no death to tear us apart. My mother hadn't been one to want children.

My father wasn't my real father and had hated me since the day I was born. There was no love lost there. I didn't even know where he was living now, nor did I care.

My friends had always been my family. Soon I would be building a family of my own here in this town. I'd make the Lawton name something to be proud of, and the house that had held so many lies, hate, and darkness would be filled with the sounds of Willa's laughter and our kids growing up happy and loved. They'd have all I didn't have. The mother neither Willa nor I had been given.

"You gonna just stand here and look at it all?" Brady asked me as he walked toward me.

I shrugged. "Depends, you got a drink?"

He smirked, then pulled out a flask from inside his jacket. "I figured we might all need a swig. This being our first rodeo with this."

I took the flask and took a swig, then handed it back. "We'll be pros by the end of the year," I told him.

"Damn right. How much longer you think it'll be before the other three get hitched?" he asked.

I inhaled deeply and scanned the crowd for the others. "I figure Ryker is next. He's gonna do some elaborate shit that makes the damn news."

Brady laughed. "Nash will be after him. He's not gonna let Tallulah get away a second time."

"And then Asa will be last. He and Ezmita need more time. They wasted a lot of it over the years. We all knew they belonged together back then. It was fucking obvious."

Brady turned to look back toward West and his mother, now walking over to the minister. "Looks like they are patching things up," he said, nodding in their direction.

"About damn time," I muttered.

"Have you heard from Willa? Do you know when they're getting here? I tried calling Riley, and it went to voice mail."

I had dropped Willa off at Brady's mom's early this morning. They'd had a day's worth of preparing. "She texted an hour ago making sure I was getting ready, but that's it."

Brady's parents drove up beside us then, and Bryony was in the backseat with some flowers in her hair. She was grinning at Brady. Never thought Brady would make such a great dad so young, but he did. He was everything my brother would never have been.

"Daddy!" Bryony squealed, seeing no one but him when she climbed out of the car wearing a white dress that was all fluffy and girly. "It's almost time!"

Brady moved forward and picked her up for a hug.

Her gaze met mine then, and the smile on her face was the one that reminded me that I had some family with same blood. The Lawton smile on that little girl had always reminded me that I wasn't the only good Lawton in this world. She was the best, even if her last name would be Higgens. I was okay with that.

I had only missed a little less than two years of Bryony's life. I still regretted it. My stupidity. I knew the pain that had caused me. I was doing all I could now to help Willa find a way to heal the same pain and regret I knew she felt over the time she'd lost with Bella. Watching them decorate Bella's room at our house and listening to them talk on the phone brought me more joy than I realized possible. As I looked at Bryony, I understood it, and I knew how lucky Willa and I were to be given second chances in life with family.

BRADY

"You're going to be a professional flower girl by the time you turn nine," I told Bryony as I set her back down on her feet. If I wrinkled her dress, my mother would have my head.

"In Gunner's wedding, I get to have a flower girl friend. We get to walk together. Willa promised we could have a playdate soon."

Willa's little sister was new to her world, but Gunner had said they had been visiting her often. She was trying to make up for lost time. Willa's mother had passed away much quicker than they had expected, about two weeks ago. Gunner hadn't said much about it other than Willa was working through it emotionally.

"You better learn the ropes, and then you can teach her," Gunner said. "She's younger than you."

Bryony nodded her head and straightened her shoulders with the acknowledgment she was older. It gave her a sense of importance. She was growing up fast, and I wished time would slow down.

"Don't you two look handsome," Mom said as she got out of the passenger seat and began straightening Bryony's hair.

"Thanks," we both replied.

"Which one of you has the flask?" my dad asked as he walked around the car.

Gunner nodded his head toward me.

"Boone!" my mother scolded my dad.

"What? It's a wedding—someone has a flask. Besides, it's your son that has it. Scold *him*," Dad replied, then held out his hand for the flask, which I put in it.

"Sorry, Mom," I apologized.

She rolled her eyes. "No, you're not."

Gunner chuckled beside me.

"Just promise me you won't be carrying one at your wedding," Mom said to me in a stern voice.

"Of course not. Gunner will," I told her, making her scowl at me.

Gunner held up his hands. "Hey, don't involve me in this. Remember the cigarettes?"

That got a laugh from Dad. Mom smirked and turned her gaze to Gunner. "You three were in the seventh grade."

"It's okay, Mom. None of us understood that you were supposed to inhale. I doubt our month of rebellious smoking did any harm to our lungs."

Gunner had stolen a pack of cigarettes from his brother. He, West, and I had thought we were the coolest kids in town, although it was a miracle we made it an entire month before we were caught. The smell alone should have given us away.

"Speak for yourself. I was inhaling," Gunner replied.

"What's 'inhale' mean?" Bryony asked.

"Okay, that's enough of the talking. Let's get you to where the wedding planner is," Mom said, directing Bryony away from us.

Dad shook his head as he looked at the two of us. "Seems like yesterday the three of you were headed to summer camp, and now here we are starting the summer with a wedding. It's crazy how fast that went. Don't blink, boys," he said, then went to follow Mom.

"There's Nash and Ryker." West nodded in their direction as they walked our way from the parking lot.

"They clean up well," I replied.

"Do you remember Ryker being so damn huge back in high school? How the hell did he explode like that?" West asked.

"Don't you remember how big he was getting his senior year? Then that first year in college he morphed into a massive beast," I said.

"Higgens, did you just call me a beast?" Ryker asked with a crooked grin.

I shrugged. "Just repeating the media."

"Can't always believe the press," he shot back at me.

It was good to be here with all of us together again so soon. Shifting my gaze back to the chairs covered in fancy covers with flowers on them, I looked among the guests for the groom. He wasn't with his mother anymore. Instead he was looking out toward the parking lot. He was ready to see his bride.

MAGGIE

The look on his face will stay with me forever. Sure, as a little girl I had imagined my wedding day, but it was a fantasy that was short-lived. My father's abusive behavior toward my mother had taken that away from me. I had wanted to be the same as everyone else so badly I'd let myself pretend we were. That all married couples fought like my parents. That all dads controlled their wives.

It wasn't until I watched him take her from this world that I let it sink in that we weren't normal. My family had never had a healthy home. We were damaged, and in my darkest place I never thought I would find a way out of that place. As much as my uncle Boone and aunt Coralee had loved me and brought me into their home, it hadn't been enough.

The night West Ashby kissed me in all his anger and pain, I began to see something worth living for. I wonder sometimes what life would have been like had I not moved to Lawton and met West. I can't imagine I would have ever found myself again. Being there for him during his darkest days pulled me out of my self-preserving world I'd withdrawn into.

My aunt Coralee asked me once why I had wanted to help West so much so that I was willing to brave the sound of my own voice again. I was willing to face my own demons.

It was because my soul and his were familiar. Something deep inside me wanted to be near him. It had made me willing to do all I could to help someone else even though I was completely broken myself.

Uncle Boone patted my hand, which was hooked inside his arm. "Her aunt Coralee and I do," he replied, then he let me go. My eyes never left West's as he reached out his hand for mine.

"I love you," he whispered as I stepped up to stand beside him.

"I love you," I replied.

Every word the minister spoke, I listened to, but my

eyes never left West's. This was our beginning. We would build a life together. He would be a loving husband and father. He was everything a little girl dreams of as the man she will marry. He was everything I had once thought didn't exist.

It was as if my mother had sent me to him. He was my perfect. Finding him in this world had made me the luckiest woman alive. Which made me think there had to be someone looking out for me. Someone who knew I needed this man.

When West turned to face me, taking both my hands in his, I felt my throat thicken before he even began the vows he had written himself. Knowing that what he said to me today was something he felt and not something that was given to him made this more intimate.

"I was lost in a darkness, and I couldn't find a light. Then you appeared. You made me want to be stronger. Your love for me saved me. Every day that has passed since that moment I realized you were the only girl I would ever love, I've managed to find more reasons to love you. More reasons to adore you. For you, I would do anything. I will cherish you and protect you. You'll never feel alone. When life gets hard and dark times happen, I'll never let you down. I'd give up everything to protect you. You are my world, the reason I breathe."

He took my right hand then and placed it over his heart. "I will always be your safety."

A truer claim had never been spoken. Because that was exactly what he was.

Acknowledgments

My editor at Simon & Schuster, Nicole Ellul, who was patient with me while I had to go back and read every one of the previous books in the series before writing each couple's future. I've enjoyed working with her again.

My agent, Jane Dystel, who I know I can turn to with any problem or issue. She's the best.

Abbi's Army ALWAYS. Y'all are what keeps me sane when I release a new book. Thanks for always supporting me.

The TikTok world for sharing this series. I love seeing the daily videos and creativity of readers. I feel as if it brings my characters to life.

My husband, Britt, who keeps the house turning when I am in a pinch. He works more than I do, but he never complains when my procrastination makes things harder.

My kids, who understand that I can't always answer their calls and text. They know when I'm writing, and they respect that.

My two older daughters, Annabelle and Ava, for giving me so much materiel to work with over the years as I wrote this series. Without them, there would be no Field Party series.

And my readers . . . without you, I wouldn't be able to write. Thank you.